THE MOUSE AND THE MAESTRO

SPIES LIKE US, BOOK 3

VANESSA GRAY BARTAL

DRY CREEK PRESS

CHAPTER 1

Jane was a nervous person. But she was also accustomed to living
in large cities, to taking care of herself and keeping safe. When
she saw the man behind her, she knew she was being followed.
What she didn't know was what to do about it.

At first she tried to lose him, quickly darting inside a shop and
hiding behind a clothes rack until she was certain he must be gone.
When she emerged from the store and saw no sign of him, she
thought she'd succeeded. And then, to her consternation, she saw him
ahead of her, paused as if he were looking at the magazine stand. Jane
knew better; he was waiting for her. *Now what?* Should she scream for
help? The only time she had ever screamed was once when an *Oxford
English Dictionary* fell on her little toe. The one that went wee-wee-
wee all the way home wee'd for certain on that day. Now if she
screamed, who would help? Worse, who would care? The falafel cart
guy? Not likely.

She passed the tattooed man, and he resumed walking behind her.
Not too close, not close enough for her to draw attention to his presence, to push him or yell at him to go away. But close enough so she
knew he was there and felt vaguely threatened. His right arm was
covered in colorful tattoos. Jane had no tattoos. Everyone she knew

had them, including her ninety-year-old neighbor who had recently gotten one on her foot. But for Jane they still signaled danger and rebellion, and Jane was neither dangerous nor rebellious. She should get the opposite of a tattoo to signal how mild-mannered and conformist she was, but the only thing she could think of was a minivan, and she was saving that until she got married and had kids.

Two blocks later, the crowds thinned and the man was still following her. Jane hurried her step, so close to work and safety she could taste it. A glance behind showed the man hurrying, too. Finally she saw the museum in the distance. She could practically smell the comforting must of artifacts from here. *Home,* she thought, so close, so easy to reach as long as she made it there before the man who was tailing her.

She darted inside and sprinted to the elevator. No way would she risk getting trapped in a stairwell with the psycho who'd been stalking behind her. The elevator was safer as long as it arrived quickly. Her finger jabbed the button again as she shot a glance over her shoulder. No one was there; she was safe.

The elevator finally arrived. Jane darted inside, breathing a sigh of relief, but as the doors began to close, a hand slid between them, almost like a horror movie. She stifled a scream as the tattooed man stepped inside and gave her a chilling smile. His arm reached out, but now she was ready. She withdrew the pepper spray from her purse and sent a pulse directly into his eyes. He dropped to the ground, writhing in agony. Jane choked as the cloud of pepper spray enveloped the elevator. Her eyes were streaming too, but it was worth it. She was safe.

The door opened onto her floor. An entire group of strangers stood staring at her, and Jane remembered why she'd been in such a hurry this morning. The team of federal agents was coming today to meet with her. One of them stepped forward and held out his hand.

"Dr. Dunbar, I'm Cameron Ridge, senior director of the team. It appears you've already met our hacker, Blue."

On the floor of the elevator, the man with the blue hair and tattoos moaned, rocking back and forth in agony, his hands clawing at his face.

Cameron Ridge turned to the blond woman standing behind him. "Hon, can you take Blue to the bathroom and get him cleaned up?"

Meekly, she stepped forward and helped the blue-haired man off the floor, putting her arm around him as they stumbled to the bathroom. Jane turned her attention to Cameron Ridge, her face flooded with heat. To deflect from her embarrassment, she focused on the next thing that grabbed her attention.

"Do you always call your employees 'hon,' Mr. Ridge?" she asked, her tone icy and affronted.

"Only the ones I'm married to, Dr. Dunbar. Why don't you take a moment to get yourself together and we'll meet in the conference room in ten," he suggested. He turned his back on her and walked away, and Jane had the sinking feeling she'd been dismissed, possibly forever.

CHAPTER 2

"Holy banshees, what is that woman's problem?" Blue asked.

"They warned us she was…different," Maggie said. She bathed Blue's eyes with cool water as he hunched over the sink like some kind of macabre beauty salon.

"I didn't do anything, I swear. I was reaching for the button to close the door, and she sprayed me. No warning, nothing. She's psychotic."

"I know," Maggie said, patting his back soothingly.

Now he groaned for a whole different reason. It wasn't ideal to have feelings for a woman who was married to another man. He was doing his best to get over her, but it went better when she wasn't touching him, caring for him, cleaning pepper juice out of his eyes.

"Maybe you need to go to the hospital," Maggie said, misinterpreting his groan of misery for continued eye pain. Eye pain was easy. He'd take it any day to heartache. He was so over feeling sad and lonely.

"I'll be fine," he assured her.

"You don't have to pretend to be okay all the time. I know something's been bothering you for a while, but you keep telling me you're fine," she said.

"I'm a hacker, Maggie. It's our nature to stuff things inside and only let them out in virtual reality. You should see my avatar. Guy never stops weeping."

She laughed, and it was another dagger in his heart. He loved to hear her laugh, to make her laugh. It was warm and infectious, like a rain shower on a warm summer day. He groaned again. He was seriously pathetic.

"Blue, you're worrying me," Maggie said, again with the back patting.

He stood, easing himself out of her reach. She handed him a wad of paper towels, and he pressed them to his eyes. "It's better, thanks." When he removed the towels from his face, she was standing a few inches away, staring at him with big, worried eyes. She grasped his forearms.

"You could go home. Ridge would understand."

"No he wouldn't, and I'll be fine, really."

She squeezed his arms. "Don't be macho."

"It's unavoidable. I'm a bubbling cauldron of testosterone." She laughed, hard. "Thanks for finding the humor in that. Be right back, going to go add more weeping to my avatar."

She let him go to clutch her stomach. "Stop it. I'm getting to that stage of laughter where I'm not going to be able to control it, and you know Ridge hates it when you make me giggle during meetings with outsiders."

"Outsiders? What are we, a cult now?"

"Blue, please," she gasped, doubling over.

Ridge pushed open the door. His eyes went first to his wife, doubled over with laughter, and landed next on Blue, standing rigidly away from her, his red eyes swollen to four times their normal size. They were giant orbs with slits for pupils. Ridge sputtered and pressed his lips together. "Everything, uh, okay in here?"

"You're laughing at how I look, huh?" Blue asked.

Ridge sputtered a little laugh and cleared his throat. "Absolutely not. That would be unprofessional, Betty Boop."

Maggie looked up at Blue. "Oh, the big eyes, Betty Boop. I'm dying." She doubled over again and this time stumbled into the wall laughing.

"Great, she's lost to us for the rest of the day, and this time it's on you," Blue said.

"I hear your words, but it's really hard to take you seriously when you look like a Muppet," Ridge said, and Maggie dropped to the floor, laughing so hard she lost the ability to support herself.

"Remember when you never talked to anyone and didn't have a sense of humor? I miss those days," Blue said to Ridge.

"Screw up this case, and you'll see them again," Ridge promised. "Are you actually okay? Do you need to go home? Because you can. That looks really painful." He sputtered again but got himself back under control.

"I'm fine," Blue said.

Maggie clutched at his calf. "Muppet. Like Sam the Eagle," she gasped before dissolving into uncontrollable laughter again.

Blue shook her off. "I'm glad you guys find so much humor in my misery."

"Please, please, please say 'It's the American way,' for me," Maggie pled, wheezing now.

"You broke her, you fix her," Blue said to Ridge, shaking Maggie off again as he sidestepped her out of the room.

"Come on, baby girl, put the stopper back on the bottle." Ridge stooped to pick Maggie up and Blue closed the door, not wanting to see what would undoubtedly be a charming resolution to their little scene. They really were adorable. If he didn't hate them together so much, he would find them delightful. As it was, their unmitigated joy in each other's presence only served to deepen his misery.

CHAPTER 3

They hated her, of course. And why wouldn't they? She had pepper sprayed one of them before the morning even began. And then she accused their leader of being a misogynist for using a term of endearment on his wife. Jane sat in the meeting room clutching a bottle of water, hands shaking, trying to get herself back under control. She had desperately hoped to go into this day with a clean slate, with no one realizing how incredibly awkward and different she was. Instead she had exposed herself to all of them within the space of five minutes. She had outed the secret herself: she was an outsider forever with no hope of fitting in.

Cameron Ridge stood at the front of the meeting room. His team became immediately silent as if he were the teacher and they the restless classroom. "Good morning, everyone. I'd like to introduce Dr. Jane Dunbar. She specializes in mid-east artifacts from the Middle Ages. She's agreed to consult with us on our current case. Dr. Dunbar, is that how you prefer to be addressed?"

Jane couldn't tell if he was making fun of her or if it was an honest question. "Jane will be fine, thank you," she replied.

"Jane, let me introduce our team. This is Maggie Ridge, my wife and our information coordinator. Maggie compiles, controls, and maintains the flow of information for each case. She'll coordinate everything you give her and put it into a workable database for us to have at our fingertips. She specializes in cross referencing which doesn't sound like much, but when you maintain as much data as we do, it comes in handy."

Maggie gave Jane a smile and a little wave. Jane gave her a nod of acknowledgement in return.

"To my left is Ethan, our field agent and a new addition to the team. He's leaving for Iraq tomorrow, so you won't see much of him. Our contact will be sporadic at best, so we like to have as much information ready to go at a moment's notice whenever he gets the chance to check in.

"On Maggie's right you'll find Babs and Ellen, our data entry specialists. You do not want to go against them in a typing contest. Spoiler alert: it will end badly for you."

The door opened and closed. Someone sat to Jane's left. Ridge smiled at the newcomer. Maggie sputtered a laugh and bit her knuckle. "And joining us is Blue Bishop, our aforementioned hacker extraordinaire. You two will be working, ah, closely together. Any questions?"

Everyone looked at Jane and she could feel her heart pounding. She shook her head.

"Great, let's get started with what we know." Cameron Ridge reached for a remote and the screen at the front of the room popped to life. "2010 began the Arab spring, a series of uprisings that aimed to overthrow oppressive regimes. I won't go into the other countless issues surrounding that because we'll be narrowing our focus to one thing: forgery.

"All the instability in the region allowed looters and gangs to raid museums and libraries, stealing priceless artifacts and selling them on the black market. At the same time, they began doing a series of forgeries and selling those, too. Over the last year, we've begun to see two disturbing patterns. One, the forgers and thieves seem to have unified into one powerful group. Two, the money from those thefts and forgeries is being funneled into multiple terror groups, one of which has recently pinged on our radar in a major way.

"And now we get to our area of combined interest. Blue's been tracking a series of posts on the dark web indicating an influx of both forgeries and real artifacts. They're in the states and flooding the market. The forgeries are good, some of the best we've ever seen. Dr. Dunbar, Jane, is one of the few people in the world who can tell the difference. She'll be assisting us as we try to get ahead of this thing. Jane, is there anything you'd like to add?"

There was a reason Jane worked with artifacts and not people. All eyes were on her again, and she felt the familiar panic creeping in. *Say something, say something, say something.* "The forgeries flooding the market are detrimental to our conservation efforts. I'll do whatever I can to help." There. Whew. She got out a complete phrase and didn't bumble it too badly.

The meeting was adjourned a moment later. She grabbed her mug of coffee and turned to go, stumbling slightly when her sweater became stuck on the corner of the chair. She didn't fall, but the motion was enough to send her hot coffee shooting out of her mug and directly into the lap of the man next to her, Blue, the tattooed guy whose eyes she'd pepper sprayed less than an hour ago.

He yelped and jumped. "Oh," Jane exclaimed, attempting to spring free to try and help. Unfortunately he leaned forward at the same time she did and, mug in hand, she clunked him in the nose. Hard.

"Oh, my, I just, I, oh…" she flapped her hands helplessly a few times before spying the open bottle of water beside her. Intending to offer it to help clean his pants she grabbed it and spun toward him. Newton's law had its way again and while the bottle stopped, the liquid inside did not. It sloshed out of the bottle and drenched the man's shirt.

Her brain went into panic mode, searching for something, anything to say. "Nice to meet you," was what it decided on.

Across the room, Maggie Ridge laid her head on the table, almost shrieking with laughter.

*L*ater, Jane sat in her office. The temptation was there to turn out the lights and rest her head on the table. Instead she kept the lights on and tried to work on clearing out her inbox, sending important messages she could no longer put off. Jane liked working with artifacts and antiquities. They were the heartbeat of her world, the entire reason she'd gone into her field. It was her bad luck as a human that working with other people also came into play.

She was bad with people. Abysmal, really. She had grown up in a different sort of family, one that moved and traveled a lot, never really allowing her to put down roots and make friends. In college she had finally warmed up to a handful of people enough to call them true friends, and they remained her only close friends to this day. She texted two of them now.

Am having the worst day in the history of time. Peed a guy's pants for him. Might die.

The first to reply was Nick, a Brit who was in the US indefinitely, currently at work on his doctorate:

Brew tea. If it's good enough for the queen, who are you to disagree? PS. Don't pee his pants with said tea.

The second reply was from Emily, Jane's roommate, a psychiatry resident currently doing her rotation at a mental institution:

There's space for you here. LMK if you need a room or lobotomy. Family/friends discount for both. Bring a friend, two for one. (Also counts for multiple personalities.)

So deep was Jane's despair their replies barely brought a smile. She set her phone aside as someone knocked on her door.

"Come in," she called.

It was the blue haired guy. Her mind went into panic mode. What was his name? *What was his name?* She should know this, especially after she hastily grabbed a stack of napkins and tried to swipe coffee off a part of his pants she should only touch after marriage. Maybe not even then. After a few swipes, he had caught her wrist and shook his head. That was when Jane finally gave up and fled the room.

"We need to go over some things," he said.

She ground her palms to her eyes. "I know. The coffee and the water and the napkins and the pepper spray. It was all…"

"Work things," he said, holding his laptop aloft.

"Oh, right. Okay."

He remained standing in the doorway, staring at her. "Is it all right if I come in?" His eyes roamed the room, probably looking for any sharp objects she might accidently impale him with.

"Yes."

He entered cautiously and sat down. "I'd like to show you some of the pictures I've been able to siphon of some of the artifacts, get your opinion on them."

"Okay," Jane said. He set the laptop on the opposite side of her desk, typed furiously a few moments, and turned the computer to face her. She reached for it, and he backed away, removing his hands before she could touch him.

She leaned in, staring at the pictures, clicking through them and tilting her head for a better view. "If these are forgeries, they're remarkable. I would only be able to tell with a hands on examination."

"A museum in Philadelphia purchased one of them. I'll see if Ridge can set up a showing."

"The head of the museum there is a friend of mine. I'll give him a call and set up a viewing," Jane said.

"One of us will need to go with you to see what we're dealing with," Blue said.

"All right," she said.

An awkward lull fell between them.

"About this morning. I'm sorry I pepper sprayed you and everything else that came after. I thought you…"

"You thought I was a murderer because I have blue hair and tats. I get that a lot," he said.

"You were following me," Jane said.

"I was not, I was merely heading here for my job."

"I didn't know that," she said.

"Because you made assumptions. Because I have blue hair and tats."

"I am five feet and three inches. I weigh a hundred and fifteen pounds on a good day. You're what, six feet, six one?"

"Six two," he said. "And, for the record, I have been to prison."

She flinched with shock.

"Oh, you're surprised by that? I thought it would have been a given in your mind."

"I think you're being a bit hard on me," she said.

"You pepper sprayed me for sharing an elevator with you," he said, pointing to his still-swollen eyes.

"Again, I'm very sorry. But I thought you were following me. I was frightened. What if you had been a killer? Should I have waited until you clubbed me over the head so I didn't come off as judgmental?"

"Whatever," Blue said. He stood to gather his laptop. Unfortunately it was the same moment Jane decided to smack it closed, smashing his fingers inside.

"Oh, come on," Blue exclaimed, withdrawing his fingers and shaking them in the air.

"You should probably go," Jane said, pressing her thumb to the middle of her forehead.

"I'm leaving, and rest assured I haven't stolen anything from your office." He collected his laptop and stormed out the door.

Jane picked up her phone and texted Emily.

If lobotomies erase memories, sign me up for two of them.

She set the phone aside and peered outside her office. No one was in the hallway. Satisfied no one was watching, she crawled under her desk and cried.

CHAPTER 4

"I hate her."

"Hate's a strong word," Maggie said. They were having their twice monthly after work outing at their favorite hangout. Blue usually had fun, but tonight he wasn't in the mood.

"You know what else is strong? Pepper spray. And hot coffee."

"The pepper spray I'll give you, but the coffee was totally an accident," Maggie replied. "And a really, really funny one." She sputtered and pressed her palm to her mouth, pushing the laughter back down.

"She's prejudiced," Blue said.

"You know you're really gleamingly white to be talking about prejudice," LuAnn interjected.

"Maybe she's not racially prejudiced, but she's prejudiced against people with colored hair and tattoos. I mean, have you seen her? She looks like a pilgrim," Blue said.

"I think she's cute," Maggie said.

Blue rubbed his hand over his eyes. They were still red and sore. "Maggie, I swear. You could be in the Gulag and talking about how Stalin is probably merely misunderstood. It's okay to say you don't like someone. It's okay to say she's a standoffish prude, an ice princess."

Maggie bit her lip, trying to hold back more words.

He poked her. "Say it."

"I do think she's misunderstood. I think she's shy and socially awkward."

"I'll give you the awkward part," Blue said, scowling. "Why are you standing up for her? She's an *outsider*." He said the last part in a scary whisper.

"So was I, not that long ago. And do I have to remind you what you thought of Ridge in the beginning? First impressions are not always correct," Maggie said.

"Okay, we were wrong about Ridge, but he never burned off my retinas with capsaicin or diminished my chances for reproduction with coffee."

"No, but he was going to. Way to ruin Christmas, Blue," Maggie said, and he grinned at her.

"You are not allowed to cheer me up after this day. Stop it. Let me wallow in my misery and loathing. Jane Dunbar is horrible, and I hate her, hate her, hate her."

Ridge finally arrived, late as usual after tying up loose ends at work. "I'm sorry to hear that because guess who's accompanying her to Philadelphia." he said, stooping to kiss Maggie before sitting down beside her.

Blue dropped his forehead onto the table with a groan. "Someone trade lives with me." *And please let it be Ridge.*

"I will," LuAnn said, wincing as she shifted in her chair. She was eight months pregnant with twins. Tonight's outing would likely be her last for a long time. "You can push these two out and then we'll trade back."

"I would, but I've been recently incapacitated by hot coffee," Blue said, his tone bitter.

"It is in your best interest to get along with Jane Dunbar," Ridge said, though not unkindly.

"Tell her that," Blue said.

"I did. She said she feels terrible about everything and she wants to start over. Clean slate."

"My slate is scalded and coffee stained," Blue said.

"Blue," Ridge said, eyes narrowing.

"Fine, Dad, whatever. I'll try to get along with the little harpy."

Ridge cleared his throat.

"I mean the little sweetheart. She's super. We're going to be BFF's. Maybe I'll go make some bracelets right now with my 3D printer. Speaking of which, I can't find her."

"I think she's at the museum," Maggie said.

"You know I only speak in terms of the virtual world, and yet you continue to mock," Blue said.

"No, that's why I mock," Maggie said.

"She has no social media footprint. None. No credit rating. No social security record. No driver's license." He looked around the table, but no one seemed to care. "Doesn't anyone find that odd?"

"That you tried to hack a new coworker? Yes," Ridge said. "Also, outside of social media, none of what you just said was legal."

"In the scheme of things, what does legality have to do with anything, really?" Blue mused.

"How was Victorville, Blue? Good enough for a return trip?" Ridge asked.

Blue sighed. He had done eighteen months in the federal penitentiary at Victorville for hacking the Defense Department's computers. He'd been a hotshot eighteen-year-old hacker, out to prove himself as the best. He'd done so, but not without a price. Who knew what might have become of him if his boss, the man who recruited him, Colonel John Caruthers, hadn't paid him a little visit all those years ago? He'd never forget The Colonel's words to him when he was a cocky, misguided nineteen year old.

Son, you have two choices: You can finish your time here and keep being stupid, or I can get you out now and you can work for me. And so Blue had left prison eighteen months ahead of schedule, moved cross country to Washington DC, and started his career in military intelligence six months before his twentieth birthday. He began at the Defense Department, shoring up security of the same place he'd hacked, and then went to the FBI before landing at the CIA and now Ridge's team. And he'd enjoyed his life immensely. Until today and Jane Dunbar.

"This is a temporary assignment and then you'll never have to see her again," Maggie consoled him. "You can do it, we're all behind you."

"Far behind you, out of the range of coffee and pepper spray," Ridge said and Maggie spit out her root beer.

"I hate you all," Blue said, but he didn't mean it. They were his second family, and he loved them, some more than others. Jane Dunbar, not at all.

CHAPTER 5

Two days later, Blue and Jane were headed to Philadelphia. Coincidentally it was Blue's hometown, but he didn't say as much to Jane. In fact, they had been in the car for an hour and neither had spoken a word.

Jane stared out the passenger window, probably making an escape plan in case he touched her. Every once in a while Blue glanced at her to see if she had moved, but she hadn't. She was like a statue. Grudgingly, Blue admitted Maggie was right; she was cute. Her features were incredibly fine and delicate. If she had a different personality, he might have said she looked like an elf or fairy. As it was she was more like a china doll—cold and untouchable.

"Thank you for driving," she said so quietly he almost didn't hear.

"You're welcome."

"Is this your car?" she asked.

"Yes," he said, bracing his hands on the wheel for the inevitable follow up question: *How does a government employee afford a Jaguar?* "I sold an app," he blurted when she failed to ask. "It's not enough to live on for life, but it was enough to buy an apartment and car and stash some away for retirement, kids college, that sort of thing."

"You have kids?" she asked.

"No, but it's never too early to plan, or so they say."

She nodded and resumed staring out the window.

"What was the app?" she asked forty minutes later.

Blue darted her a smile. "Were you thinking of that all this time?"

She smiled in return and tapped her temple. "The introvert brain is slow to process."

"It's called Threeple. You know that game Six Degrees of Kevin Bacon? It's like that. You put in any person and it tells you how many degrees you are away from them based on common friends on social media and known shared ancestors."

"You made Threeple? That's my favorite app," she said.

"Really?" he asked, his glance darting to her again.

"It saved me from marrying my cousin."

He blinked at her. "You're joking." It was hard to tell because her tone and expression were deadpan.

She nodded. "Congratulations, though. That's amazing. I barely even know how to use apps." She held her flip phone aloft for his inspection.

From an early age, he had lived all of his life online. He had never personally met anyone who didn't have a smart phone or social media account. "Do you have a driver's license?" The fact that she was completely off the radar unnerved him. It was one more way in which he had no idea how to relate to her.

"No."

"Why not?"

"I've never lived anywhere I felt I needed one," she said.

They lapsed into silence again. Blue rested his hand on the console, not realizing her hand was already there. She jumped at the contact and withdrew her hand.

Blue put his hand back on the wheel, gripping it tightly. "You know, tattoos aren't contagious."

"No, I, it's not, I…"

"Forget it. We're here."

Blue parked. They made their way through the museum's security until at last they landed in the presence of the man they'd come to see, in what Blue presumed to be his lab. The man turned to survey them, and Blue took stock. He was young and professional looking with unruly brown hair and ubiquitously geeky glasses. He straightened and offered his hand to Jane without a smile.

"Dr. Dunbar."

Jane returned the formal shake. "Dr. Stevens."

Blue refrained from rolling his eyes. They were as cold and stiff as he'd imagined they'd be. This visit was going to be a laugh riot, but at least seeing her with a friend had done nothing to dispel his uptight image of her. And then Dr. Stevens used the hand he still held to yank Jane hard against his chest.

"Give us a kiss, Jane."

"Absolutely," Jane replied. She stood on her toes, but instead of reaching for his lips ducked out of his grasp, hopped on his back, and kissed his cheek.

He laughed. "Get off, you little monkey."

Jane slid down. "Speaking of monkeys, where's yours?"

Dr. Stevens handed her a bowl of fruit. "You know what to do."

Jane picked up the fruit and shook it. "Kiko, treats."

A monkey appeared as if from nowhere, perched on her shoulder, and reached for the fruit. "You have to pay the toll," she said, holding the fruit out of reach. She extended her lips, the monkey kissed them, and she gave him the fruit.

"Sure, the monkey you kiss on the lips," Dr. Stevens said.

"So, you have a monkey," Blue said, the first time he'd spoken since they arrived.

"It's good PR for the museum. Jane used to have a monkey, too, didn't she tell you?"

Blue shook his head, eyeing the monkey warily. They were in a lab, after all. Had no one besides him watched *Outbreak*? He held out his hand to the doctor. "Blue Bishop."

"Charles Stevens. Sorry, I got so caught up with delight at seeing Jane again I lost track of the introductions."

"You were telling me about Jane's monkey. Was this recently?" Exactly how weird was she?

"No, she was, what, nine?"

"Eight," Jane corrected.

"You guys go back a ways," Blue said. And yet the man still seemed to like her. Strange.

"Our families were in Africa for a while together," Jane said.

"How is the family?" Charles asked.

"Well, thanks."

"Is your dad still…?"

"Yes," Jane said, hasty to cut off whatever he was about to say.

"It's good to see you, Jane. It's been too long," Charles said warmly. To Blue he added, "Did she tell you we skinny dipped together?"

"Still when I was eight. And you were eleven, you corrupting perv."

"Your sister dragged me into it," Charles replied.

"That sounds about right," Jane said, smiling. The monkey grabbed another grape and skittered away. "Right, I guess we should get down to business."

"What's this all about? Your message was so cryptic," Charles said.

Blue tensed. Ridge had warned Jane not to reveal anything about their case, to say as little as possible. How would she handle deception?

She rolled her eyes. "You know how it is. We heard a whisper of forgery at the Smithsonian and Harrison went into paranoia overdrive. He has a cicada on order from Morocco, and it's making him antsy. He wanted me to check your new purchase to make sure it's legit."

"Harrison. So paranoid," Charles agreed, and they shared a smile.

"Thanks so much for fitting me in on such short notice."

"What are ex-boyfriends for?" he asked.

"One date does not a boyfriend make," she said. "Add that to the fact that you never called me again, and I think anything outside the realm of friendship between us is dead and buried."

"But the past has a way of coming back to life. If it didn't, our jobs would be meaningless," Charles said.

"The artifact," Jane said, redirecting.

"Right, yes. Let me retrieve it. I'll be right back." He walked out of the room leaving Blue and Jane in awkward silence.

"Sorry if we seem incredibly non-professional to you. As you said, we go back a long way," Jane said.

"It's fine," Blue said. What he wanted to say was that it humanized her. For the first time since he met her, he was picturing her as something other than a puritanical scold.

"This is going to take a while. You could go and come back, if you like," she said.

He would like that very much, but Ridge, anticipating that Blue would want to make a break for it, had forewarned him. *Stick to her like glue. Closer, even, like duct tape. She doesn't leave your sight. Don't ditch her, not even if she tells you to.* The instruction had been…strange. They were at the beginning of their investigation, not in a hot zone. If not for his serious expression, Blue might have thought Ridge was pulling his leg to torture him.

"I'll be fine," Blue said, withdrawing his laptop from his messenger bag.

"Oh, I used to know the wifi password here. Let me see if I can remember," she said.

He smiled. "I'm good, thanks."

"Oh, that's right. Computers are kind of your thing."

"Me hacker, you Jane," he said before he could stop himself.

"Wow. People have said that line to me an untold amount over the years, but none quite so odd as that one."

He smiled a little. "I do what I can."

She smiled in return and then Charles was back with a giant box on a wheeled cart. Jane's face lit, at the sight of the box, not the man. The two were soon lost in examining the thing in the box.

"Would you like to see?" Jane asked Blue, catching him by surprise.

"Um, sure," he said, standing to cross the room. "What am I looking at?"

"It's an alabaster canopic jar," Jane said.

"And that is…"

"During the mummification process, the internal organs were placed in these containers in order to preserve them for the afterlife."

"How old is it? Assuming it's real, I mean," Blue said.

"This one appears to be from the Eleventh Dynasty, approximately 2000 years BC. You see how the lid is plain? In later times they were carved to look like humans and then four gods."

"Four thousand years old?" Blue stuttered.

"Yes," Jane said. She had dedicated her life to artifacts, and yet she never lost her awe. She was touching something that ancient Egyptians might have touched. The sensation always left her a bit woozy. "If this is a forgery, it's spectacular."

"Can you carbon date it?" Blue asked. They looked at him as if he'd just asked to be tickled by caterpillars.

"It's stone," Jane said.

"Please don't make me admit I have no idea the significance of that," Blue said.

"You can't carbon date stone, only things that were once alive. But that brings up an interesting point—a forger would definitely know that and choose stone for that purpose," Jane said. She returned her attention full time to examining the jar, and Blue knew he was dismissed. He returned to his comfort zone, the virtual world.

Many, many hours later, after a scanty lunch of rabbit food, Jane was finished. She removed her gloves and set them aside.

"Charles, I believe it's a fake," she said quietly, sadly.

"No," Charles said, his knees almost giving way.

To Blue it was merely a jar, but he could guess the implications went much deeper for a couple of museum geeks whose livelihood depended on authenticity. "Why do you think so?" Charles asked.

Jane reached for a laptop and turned it to face him. "Here, this spot from the electron microscope. It captured a brush stroke." Blue came to stand over her shoulder. After so many hours, it was kind of exciting to hear the result.

"Where?" he asked. He saw nothing out of the ordinary in the ultra-magnified picture.

"Here." She picked up a pen and touched the tip to the screen. He hunched closer, squinting. Doing so brought him in direct contact with her body. She did the jumping and flinching thing, and he bit down on his frustration.

"Hmm," he said, easing away from her. Even here, in her comfort zone, she couldn't warm up to him.

"Also there's the lid. The fit it's…not right."

"I have to admit that caused me a bit of concern, too, but I so badly wanted this to be legit," Charles said. He scrubbed his hand over his face looking sad and defeated.

"I'm sorry," Jane said, resting her hand on his arm.

He pulled her close and hugged her. "I know, it stinks for all of us."

Blue watched her to see how she'd react to him, but she was all-in on the hug, wrapping her arms around him and pressing her ear to his heart. Charles Stevens had no tattoos, of course. "It was an amazing forgery, possibly the best I've ever seen," she whispered. "I know it's bad timing, but do you think you can get me in to New York? I don't have a connection there."

"I'll make some calls and let you know," he promised. He kissed the top of her head. "Thanks for trying to let me down easy."

"I wish I had better news," she said. She gave him a final squeeze and stepped out of his embrace.

CHAPTER 6

"You're not a vegetarian are you?" Blue asked as soon as they were back in the car.

"No, why?"

"How do you feel about grabbing a cheesesteak before we head back to DC?" he asked. He hadn't had one since the last time he was home, and his craving could no longer be denied, especially after such a light lunch.

"That's fine, whatever you'd like," she said. She sounded tired. He should probably hustle her straight home, but they had to eat. It might as well be delicious.

He took her to his favorite place, well off the beaten tourist track. "Can you do me a favor?" she said.

"What's that?" he asked, his tone wary.

"Can you order for me? I'm going to run to the restroom."

"What do you want?" he asked.

"Whatever you're having will be fine," she said.

After she escaped to the bathroom, he remembered that she also went right before they left the museum. Either she had a tiny, nervous bladder or she was faking.

The line at the restaurant was long, giving him a lot of time to think. Maybe too much because by the time it was his turn to order, he had become suspicious of Miss Jane Dunbar. Her words rose up to condemn her. A good forger would have to know a lot about her subject. Who better than a woman with a doctorate? And she had no footprint. The only other people he knew who didn't were spies and top tier military guys like Ethan and Ridge. Their lives had been erased, making them untraceable. Maggie and Amelia were the same, thanks to their marriages. If they had children, the same protection would be granted to them. Guys like himself found it too easy to prey on people using their digital footprint. He could find out anything about anyone. Except Jane Dunbar.

She reappeared coincidentally as their food arrived. What had she been doing all that time in the bathroom? Reaching out to contacts? Setting up another deal?

"Feeling okay?" he asked.

"Yes, thank you. But I am hungry. This looks and smells amazing, thank you." Her smile was gentle, but maybe that was all part of the act. Suck in innocent dupes by pretending to be innocent herself and then—WHAM!—take them out when they least suspect it. Though, if she were a forger, she'd probably be more used to dealing with people who looked like him. Maybe she'd had a bad run in with someone who had tats and a dye job and he had merely gotten caught up in her vendetta.

"Everything okay?" she asked, and he realized he was standing at the pickup line staring at her. He gave himself a mental shake. It was possible his dislike of her was causing his imagination to run away. She was a highly esteemed anthropologist who worked for one of the most prestigious museums in the world. That alone made it unlikely she was a forger. Or did it?

"Yes," he said decisively, leading the way through the crowd to a table. They sat and he forced himself not to devour the cheesesteak like an emaciated wolverine, even though that was what he wanted to do. The restaurant had always been his favorite and his choice for every birthday and special occasion with his family.

"Does this bring back memories?" Jane asked, and he blinked at her, shocked.

"Yes, but how did you know I'm from Philly?"

"I read your bio," she said.

"Oh," he drawled. Ridge had given her a printout to help acquaint her with their team. It never occurred to him she actually read it.

Her phone buzzed with a text. She checked it, smiled, and sent a reply. Would she smile like that if the message was from one of her contacts? Perhaps, if the price was high enough.

She ate her sandwich as she did everything else—delicately, somehow even managing to not get messy. Blue, meanwhile, looked like he played the kissing game with a jar of Cheez Whiz. But she ate every bite of the huge sandwich.

"Thank you so much for that," she said when the meal was over. "It was amazing. I'll definitely come back, next time I'm here."

"You're welcome," he said. "Quick question, do you mind if we swing through a car wash so I can try to get the dried cheese off my face?"

She laughed, a tinkling little sound so delightfully unexpected that he smiled what was possibly the first real and whole smile he'd given her since he met her. She stopped short and looked at him and then promptly ran into a wall.

"Are you okay?" he asked.

"I'm fine," she assured him, but her hand was covering one eye. He led her to a bench outside the restaurant, sat her down, and crouched to inspect her.

"Let me see," he said, when she stubbornly retained the grasp on her face. He tugged her wrist, thinking as he did so that it was the first time she didn't flinch away from him. Apparently all it took for her to be comfortable around him was possible brain damage and vision loss.

"That's going to leave a mark," he said, inspecting the little purple spot on her cheek. It would likely swell and hurt for the next day or two. "Let's see if we can get you some ice for the ride home."

She said nothing, and in fact she seemed not to be blinking. It was as if someone had turned the lights off in her head, and he began to fear maybe something actually had happened to her brain.

"Are you okay?" he asked.

"Yes, I, I…" her gaze fell to his hand resting on her leg.

Oh. That was it. She couldn't stand him touching her. He snatched his hand back, the angry roar filling his chest again. For one moment he had fooled himself into thinking she was human, that she saw him as more than a guy with body art and blue hair. But he was wrong. She was as cold and uppity as he had first assumed.

"No, I," she tried again and then floundered.

"It's fine," he snapped. He started to stand when her hands reached out and captured his face. Slowly, she brought it closer to hers. She closed her eyes and kissed him, long and slow and deep, so that when it was finished, Blue was the one with a scrambled brain.

"Sorry," she whispered when the kiss was over, and then she kissed him again, drawing his face to hers again, while Blue remained too shocked to do anything more than let it happen. "Sorry," she added again, though her thumb slid gently over his bottom lip and she leaned forward and touched her lips lightly to his once more, no hands this time. Then she sat back. "Again, sorry. We should probably go before I do it again."

"Okay," Blue said. His voice sounded tinny and strained, even to him. What in the name of anime had just happened to him? No woman had ever randomly kissed him like that and, if they had, it would have been less surprising than Jane being the first. She was so… He was going to say standoffish, but that seemingly no longer applied. Different. Yes, she was very, very different. *Try looking in a mirror sometime,* his treasonous inner voice reminded him. He prided himself on different. Why did it bother him when he encountered it in someone else? Was it possible he had been guilty of reverse prejudice? That he judged Jane for her upright demeanor and unassuming style?

CHAPTER 7

Have now kissed the guy whose pants I peed.

Jane sent the text to Emily in the silent awkwardness of the car. It was the only barrier between her and waves of mortification. Without the distraction, she would surely erupt into the tears that, even now a half hour later, threatened to overwhelm her. She had always cried easily, and she hated it. Tears seemed to be hotwired into every one of her emotions—angry? Cry. Sad? Cry. Frustrated? Cry. Kiss a stranger on a whim? Cry, or try hard not to.

Go you. Is he cute? Emily texted in reply.

Jane sneaked a glance at Blue who stared raptly through the windshield.

Definitely yes. But it was filled with signature Jane awkwardness and bad timing.

Oh, Jane. Only you, Emily replied. *Come home and I'll slip some Klonopin in your tea.*

Jane smiled, albeit slightly. *My favorite bedtime snack,* she replied before stuffing her phone in her pocket. She didn't have to be told it would come off doubly crazy to kiss a man and then spend the next two hours of traffic texting on her phone. But without Emily as a buffer, however tenuous, she had nothing to do but think. *What is wrong with me?* It wasn't the first time she'd had the thought, and it wouldn't be the last. She seemed unable to function in normal society. Granted, she'd had an unusual upbringing with unusual parents, but her sisters did all right. They were social creatures, fully able to function among other humans. It was only Jane who had seemingly never been able to maintain a normal conversation that didn't involve her job. Give her an artifact, and she could lecture for hours, and often did, in the course of her work. But put her one on one with another person and ask her to delve into the world of small talk, and she became a blabbering, blithering idiot. And apparently now she kissed people at random. *Great, I was really hoping to add another quirk in there to entrench my status as a pariah.*

What was even worse was that Blue had spent the last few hours watching her interact with Charles, one of only a handful of men on the planet she felt comfortable enough to flirt with. She and Charles went back decades. He was one of the only people who knew how she grew up, who understood how it was with her dad. She had a comfort level with him she had only with members of her family. And it was her bad luck Blue had to witness it. Maybe he thought her bi-polar. How else to explain her split personality that was so standoffish and awkward with him and so warm and affectionate with Charles?

She would have to try to explain. It would undoubtedly make everything worse, but she couldn't say nothing. So she thought for a long, long time and tried to put together workable sentences. After practicing the reasonable little speech in her head a few times, she opened her mouth and tried to begin.

"You're really cute," she blurted the phrase that had been in absolutely zero parts of her rehearsed speech. She doubled over, touching her forehead to her knees.

"Are you okay?" Blue asked.

Jane held up a finger, took a deep breath, and sat up. "I get very anxious around new people. Bear with me." She took another breath. "Okay, here we go. There's this running dialogue in my head that tries to tell me things. Usually it tries to tell me I'm someone I'm not. Tonight, for instance, it tried to tell me I'm the kind of woman who can kiss an attractive stranger and get away with it. But I think we both know I'm not that person. So I'm really sorry for crossing that line with you. It was a whim, and I clearly can't do whims."

"I'm going to come back to that in a minute, but for now I have to tell you some bad news."

Cheeks flaming, she forced herself to look at him. What could be worse than what she'd already said and done?

"We picked up a tail."

"Oh."

"Find me a detour."

Jane sprang to attention and began looking around. "Where is your atlas?"

Blue sputtered a laugh. "I was talking to the car."

"I've located your detour," the car responded in a smooth computerized voice.

"Has the car been eavesdropping on us this whole time? Because I'm not sure I'm comfortable with the OnStar people knowing how awkward I am and making judgments."

He laughed again, but his eyes slid to the rearview mirror.

"Should I call the police?" she asked.

"Bad news, Jane. I kind of am the police." He mashed his foot on the accelerator, gunning it to a hundred as he wove in and out of traffic. The car behind them kept pace for a while, but eventually Blue shook them off. Then he did a U-turn on the divider, doubled back, got off the interstate, and took the alternate route the computer had provided. The tail didn't find them again.

"Who do you think that was?" she asked. She seemed unnaturally calm, and Blue's earlier suspicions returned. From what he knew of her, she was high anxiety. Yet they'd just endured a high-speed car chase on one of the busiest freeways in the country and she sat calmly still, her hands folded in her lap.

"I have no idea. The people who know what we're working on are few," he said, his eyes darting to hers again.

"I hope it's no one at the Smithsonian who leaked it," she said, a tiny bit of worry easing back into her tone.

"Me, too," he said, but he was thinking of her. "So, an atlas. Are you by chance a defrosted cavewoman?"

"Confession: I have never used GPS."

"Never?"

"Never. My job deals with artifacts and relics thousands of years old, so to me maps seem new. And I grew up in places without a lot of technology. I never learned to depend on it. But I'm aces at reading a map."

"It sounds like you had an interesting childhood," he noted.

"My parents are old school in their beliefs about childrearing. They wanted us to be intelligent, capable, resilient. In fact, they were so adamant about it that even after my dad came to the states for his job, my mom stayed a few extra years in Africa to give us a different sort of upbringing. My mom homeschooled us, and my dad taught us things you learn outside of school. He had three daughters, so he wanted us to be safe and not dependent on anyone else, especially the government."

"He doesn't trust the government?" Blue asked.

Jane's smile was wry. "He has a complicated relationship with the government."

Interesting. It kind of sounded like her dad was either an anti-government nutcase or a criminal.

The remainder of the ride was uneventful and soon they were back in DC. "You can let me out in front of my building. You'll never find parking," Jane said.

"All right," Blue agreed. He double parked in the road, miraculously free of other traffic for the moment. Jane reached for the door, but he rested his hand on her leg. "I need to double check something with you."

She turned attentively in his direction, and he was momentarily distracted. Okay, maybe she was a bit more than cute. Maybe she was pretty, and her eyes were...*Focus*. "The reason you've been so jumpy when we touch is not because you find me scary and repulsive."

"That is correct," she said, her tone soft and shy.

"And in fact some might say you find me attractive," he continued.

"Some might," she said, smiling gently. "That first day, when you followed me, I did find you scary, but I honestly would have no matter who the man was. My dad taught me to be alert and attuned to danger. But after I realized you weren't, in fact, a serial killer, I realized you were…quite cute. So apparently my reaction to serial killers and attractive men is exactly the same. Good thing I never encountered Ted Bundy. I probably would have accidentally wandered off a cliff."

He laughed, and her smile widened. She reached for the door again, but his hand was still on her leg. "I need to say one more thing."

"Yes?" she asked, face alight with curiosity as she turned back toward him. He leaned in and kissed her until someone honked behind him, and it was time to let go.

"Turns out I am the kind of guy who can kiss an attractive stranger on a whim and get away with it." His thumb brushed her cheek, and she blinked at him.

"Oh," she whispered. "Okay. Thank you. Good happy night." Her words registered and she opened the car door, bolting out of sight.

CHAPTER 8

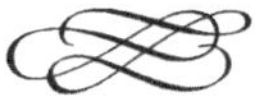

"Call Ridge," Blue directed his car. A moment later, his boss's voice rang over his Bluetooth speakers.

"Every time you call at night, it's bad news," Ridge greeted him.

"How many times is there good news in our job? Do you think I'm going to ever call and say the terrorists found the Lord and surrendered?"

"I'm keeping the dream alive," Ridge replied. "What's up?"

"The artifact was a fake, and we picked up a tail outside of Philly."

"What?" Ridge exclaimed.

"I lost them, but the fact remains it's not good."

"No, it's very, very not good," Ridge agreed. "The pool of people who know about this case is extremely small."

"About that, what do we actually know about Jane Dunbar?"

"Enough. She's clean."

"But how do we know?"

"We know. And not only is she clean, but she's a high-value target."

"An anthropologist? Why?" Blue asked.

"It's classified."

"You know we have the same clearance," Blue reminded him. In fact Blue was certain he'd dealt with more secrets in his time than Ridge had. In the scheme of things, Ridge was a newbie.

"It's a different kind of classified."

"What other kind is there?" Blue asked.

"The personal kind. Take my assurance she's clean and keeping her safe is your number one priority. In fact, Blue, your life depends on it."

"Okay, that's not cryptic at all," Blue drawled.

"What in our job isn't cryptic?" Ridge asked.

"You have a point there."

"How did it go between you two, other than the tail? I take it you're both still alive and no one got maced or Tasered."

"No, it was fine. She's, ah, growing on me. A little."

"Good. Maggie likes her."

"Maggie likes everyone," Blue said.

"No, she sees the potential in everyone; there's a difference. But Jane she likes. She thinks she's shy and misunderstood."

"She may be," Blue said. And she also might be a master forger. Despite Ridge's assurances, he wasn't ready to let go of his suspicion yet, even if it was the best kiss he'd had since before he cared to remember. "Hello?" he tried, but Ridge was gone without saying goodbye. Again. "Good talk, boss," he muttered and turned the car toward home.

The next morning, coffee for Jane was more of a necessity than a habit. She eased into the chair of the conference room at the museum, trying to slip under the radar and go unnoticed as usual. The chair beside her squeaked. She peeked out of the corner of her eye and saw Blue scoot close to the table. He gave her a tentative smile.

She leaned toward him and whispered. "Guaranteed spill proof," tapping the lid of her travel mug.

He snickered a laugh, drawing the attention of Maggie and Ellen across from them. Maggie raised her eyebrows. Blue shrugged. She reached for her phone and sent a text. His phone pinged and he texted in return. Jane was dying to know what they were saying.

Ridge stood and once again the room came to attention. Jane had no idea what his secret was, but he might consider teaching high school when his career in military intelligence was over. He filled the team in on the artifact from yesterday.

"Maggie and Blue have created this database for us that overlays known forgery sales with known terror cells. As you can see the pings radiate from DC and Philadelphia. Curiously we haven't discovered any overlap in New York, which tells us either we haven't caught it yet or our forger is someone local."

Beside her Blue shifted in his chair. Ridge continued.

"Tomorrow Jane and Blue head to New York for a couple of days. Jane will be checking a few artifacts and Blue will be running intel on her contacts there. Whoever our forger is, he or she is unsettlingly familiar with the dark web. Judging by the language the person has been using online, it appears to be the same person or possibly someone with an extensive knowledge of the forgeries and the realm in which they belong. After my conversations with Jane, I'm convinced it would either have to be someone who has been educated in Egyptology or spent enough time in the field to have a working knowledge of artifacts. These are detailed, impeccable forgeries that, again according to Jane, must have taken months if not years to create. Jane, can you expand more on that, please."

He had warned her he would call on her today, and she felt better prepared. She had notes, and her coffee had a spill proof lid in case she went Nutty Professor again. "Thank you, Agent Ridge," she remembered to say as he sat and handed her the floor. "The best replicas are not complete fakes. They employ a mix of old materials and new techniques. For instance, someone might purchase a piece of material that's a few centuries old for relatively few dollars, embellish it to look a few millennia old. They would then be able to sell it for hundreds of thousands, if not millions, of dollars. Unfortunately as our detection methods have gotten better, so have their forgeries. They're sophisticated and, as Agent Ridge said, take a vast and working knowledge of the subject in question. And even then they sometimes squeak through the vetting process. I'll not bore you with the details of how many fakes are on display, even here at the Smithsonian, because I know your concern lies in the flow of where the money is going and what it's being used for. Suffice it to say it's a sophisticated operation being carried off by someone incredibly intelligent."

"Thank you, Jane," Ridge replied, standing again. "In addition to our work here, Ethan has been tracking a smuggler in Iraq who we believe may have ties to our forger. I'll let you know as soon as we have more on that front. Thank you everyone."

The meeting was adjourned. Jane closed her laptop and made sure her sweater wasn't stuck before she tried to stand this time. "When would be a good time to meet, Jane, and discuss our trip?" Blue asked.

"I'm available now, if that works for you," Jane replied. The team wasn't sticking around the museum. They had their meetings there as a courtesy to her schedule and then returned to their office a mere five blocks away.

"Now is perfect," Blue said. He strapped his messenger bag over his shoulder and followed her to her office. She closed the door, and they sat with her behind the desk and him on the opposite side.

"Before we begin, may I say one thing?" Jane asked.

"Absolutely," he replied.

"You must think I'm psychotic."

"That wouldn't have been my word, no," he said.

"No, it's okay, you can say it. First I pepper sprayed you for daring to step onto an elevator with me. Then I fell all over myself like a puppy viewing snow for the first time. And then I kissed you. Last night I had a chance to go over my behavior, and I'm so incredibly embarrassed. You're trying to do a job here, an important job, and I don't want to stand in the way of that. Please, can we forget everything that's happened and begin again?"

"If you'd like," he said. He held out his hand to her. "Blue Bishop."

"Jane Dunbar," she replied, smiling. She extended her hand and bumped her coffee but caught it before it fell. "Now, let's talk about New York, shall we?"

"Let's shall," Blue agreed. He opened his laptop, and they got to work.

CHAPTER 9

Later that night, Jane let herself into her apartment and saw Emily and Nick sitting at opposite ends of the couch, each with a book in hand. She made her way over to them and plopped onto the couch, her head in Emily's lap, her feet in Nick's.

"Stick a fork in me."

"Another day of adulting down, a few thousand or so to go," Nick said mildly.

"No, I give up. I'm going to start a blog and fully embrace agoraphobia," Jane said.

"You'll need a cat," Emily informed her.

"And a computer. Also the ability to use a computer," Nick added.

"I'm going to write an old-school blog on paper, Emily Dickinson style. Then I'll get you guys to post it to flagpoles and bulletin boards to garner followers. Then, after the money starts rolling in, I'll hire newsies to distribute."

"I hear print's going to make a comeback, but only if electricity goes out everywhere on earth forever," Nick said.

"And now we wait," Jane said, and he looked up from his book to toss her a smile.

"I take it things didn't go so well with the guy. What happened this time, Janie? Did you accidentally toss him into a meat grinder?" Emily asked.

"Guy, what guy?" Nick asked.

"Jane likes a boy at work. It's going in typical Jane fashion."

"Oh, bother. Is he in a full body cast yet?" Nick asked, returning his attention to his book.

"You survived me," Jane said, tapping him with her foot.

"Barely," he replied, pinching her toe.

"It went okay," Jane said when Emily nudged her. "I told him I want to start over again."

"And forget the kisses?"

"And forget the kisses," Jane agreed.

"Wait, there were kisses already? You made out with a guy at work? We never made out at work," Nick said, his eyes narrowing.

"We never worked together," she said.

"Is the Smithsonian hiring? Because I'm open to a career change if it means we get to make out," he said.

"You remember we're broken up, right?"

"Yes, but we never had our rebound fling," he said. "Everyone's entitled to at least one, and I feel incredibly cheated."

"Shh," Emily said, putting up a hand. "Be pathetic and needy on your own time. I want to hear about the guy. And, for the record, you guys have gotten back together and broken up so many times no one keeps track anymore."

"Seven," Nick said, grinning. "I keep track."

"Eight," Jane disagreed. "You always forget the second time freshman year."

"Oh, quite," he said, gazing off into the distance.

"Anyway," Jane said, returning her attention to Emily, "I want to get this assignment over with and move on with my life. Nothing is going to come of it, and I've already made a fool of myself. Repeatedly."

"How do you know nothing is going to come of it?" Emily asked. "This guy could be the love of your life."

"Pardon me, hello, genuine love of her life sitting right here.

College sweetheart, remember? Do ten years of off and on dating mean nothing to you people?" Nick said, but they ignored him.

"I barely know him," Jane said. "I mean, he's cute and funny and sweet and smart and has a totally cool funky vibe that intrigues me, but otherwise I barely know him."

"Basically you like everything about him, but you're scared to put yourself out there because you're Jane."

"Should I leave money on the nightstand for that analysis, Doctor?" Jane asked.

Emily grinned. "That was a freebie, but you can buy me dinner tonight, if you like."

"Let's get pizza," Nick piped up.

"If we're going out, I need to shower," Emily said, scooting from beneath Jane. When she was safely out of the room, Nick set aside his book and gathered Jane into his lap.

"Let's make out," he suggested.

"No," Jane said.

"Why not?"

"Because you've cheated on me three times with three different people. My psychiatrist made me see returning to you is a form of self-harm, a fear I'll never find anyone better, a pull toward the familiar."

"Stupid Emily," he muttered.

"She's not wrong, you know. You and I, we're better off as friends, due to your complete faithlessness as a boyfriend. I've finally accepted that, and I no longer hate you for hurting me."

"I love you, Jane, you know I do."

"I do, in fact, know that."

"And because I love you, I'm about to impart a painful truth on you: You're a complete coward, and you shouldn't be. If you like this guy, total loser though I'm sure he is, then you should go for it. Put yourself out there. Stop hiding. Show him the real Jane. If you do, I promise you'll blow him away."

"How do you know I'm hiding?" she asked.

"Because I know you, and I love you, now kiss me quick before

Emily comes back."

"Oh, no," Jane said.

"What?"

"You and Emily were making out before I got home. That's why you were sitting so far apart pretending to read. And now you're scared and trying to deflect your attraction to her."

"I should not be this easy to read," Nick said.

"Please, Nick, please don't do the thing. Don't hurt Emily. There's enough heartbreak in the world. Be lovely, be genuine, be the guy I know you actually are deep, deep, *deep* down inside. Please." She clasped her hands together under her chin.

"I'll try. No promises." He kissed her forehead and let her go. She eased off his lap and picked up Emily's book, not at all sure how she felt about the possibility of her two best friends getting together. What if they forgot her in their mad desire to be together? Worse, what if they broke up and couldn't stand to be together?

"When do we get to meet the guy?" Nick asked.

"He's picking me up tomorrow morning. Please be nice and normal. He is not my boyfriend. He merely has the unfortunate luck to be my crush, and you know from experience what that's like."

"Yeah, but I also know the end result, and it's pretty great, Jane." He reached out and squeezed her hand.

"I should probably go pack," she said.

"Let me help you," Nick said.

"You want to help me pack?" she clarified.

"Yes. I know what looks good on you. Come on." He took her hand, led her to her bedroom, and began sifting her wardrobe.

"This is weird," Jane said.

"This is not weird. Friends consult each other over what to wear all the time," Nick said.

"But you're more than my friend. There are all the other layers."

"Consider this a new layer—fashion consultant."

"How come you never cared what I wore when we were together?" she asked.

"Who says I never cared? I judged you incessantly," he said.

"Maybe those could be the thoughts you reject before they come out of your mouth," Jane suggested.

"You dress like a puritan, Janie."

"I work at a museum, Nick, not a strip club."

"There's no law saying you can't do both. Think of the money you could make with a second job. Where's the dress you wore for our college graduation?" he asked.

"On the left with the other summer clothes. But it's sleeveless, I can't wear that."

"You can with this sweater," he said, fishing them out and tossing them on the bed.

"Oh, that's actually really cute together."

"I know. How about that pink dress I like with the little horses on it, the one with the brown leather belt?"

"How do you know my clothes this well? I don't even remember that dress. It's in the middle, but it's totally wrong for work."

"It's really not. Here, pair it with this jean jacket at night for going out." He tossed those items on the bed as well.

"What shoes?" she couldn't stop herself from asking.

"These ankle boots." He withdrew the boots from her closet and tossed them beside the bed.

"How are you doing this?" she asked.

"You know art is the thing I'm getting a PhD in, so I spend sort of a lot of time thinking about color and composition. You should also change your hair."

She made a wounded sound and touched her tresses. "But I've had this hairstyle since I was fifteen."

"As someone who started dating you when you were seventeen, darling, I know," he said.

He picked out another outfit for her and turned his attention to her jewelry. "Wear the beaded necklace I made for you with this one."

"I can't wear the necklace you made for me with another man."

"Of course you can. I use the wallet you bought me when I'm with other women."

"Yeah, but you made it," she said, holding the necklace aloft to admire it.

"The necklace and I both want you to be happy," he insisted. He took the necklace from her, tossed it onto the pile of clothes, and plopped down beside her on the bed. They linked arms. "What's he like?"

"Do you really want to know?" she asked.

"In theory, yes."

"He's a website design consultant," she said, using the cover story Ridge had provided for her. Blue's job was classified.

"Poor," Nick coughed into his hand.

"No, he sold an app," Jane said.

"Which one?"

"Threeple."

Nick sat up. "Are you joking? I love that one."

"Really?"

"Yes, it's an amazing ice breaker. Here, I'll show you." He pulled out his phone, touched the Threeple app, and it sprang to life. "I'll put in me and give me a name."

"Martha Stewart," Jane suggested.

"Martha Stewart," he agreed, typing in her name. "Look, my grandma was next door neighbors with her cousin so we're three people apart. And if I put in me and Em." He held up the phone for her because it made a little party noise of celebration. "It does that whenever you have a first gen connection to someone, no separation. I'd put you in but, you know, you're off the grid and whatnot."

"That's kind of cool, actually. Seeing all the different ways you're connected to people."

"What's the guy's name? I'll put him in and see if we're connected."

"Blue Bishop," she replied. Nick gave her the side eye.

"Real name?"

"Real name. And he has blue hair and tattoos from here to here." She touched his shoulder and wrist.

"Alrighty then," Nick said. He entered the name and gasped.

"What?" Jane said, tensing.

"That's so cool. It's a hidden Easter egg. When you put his name in it brings up a picture of a wizard and tells you not to pay any attention to the man behind the curtain. Awesome. Now I really want to meet him."

"Maybe you should go to New York with him," she suggested.

"I'd show him a good time," Nick said, and she laughed. "You should too, Jane. Let him see the real you, the fun you."

"You know it's not up to me. I hear normal words in my head, but then they come out like gobbledygook, like English is my second language and awkwardness is my first."

"Anytime you get in a jam, pretend he's me," Nick advised.

"Are you suggesting anytime I don't know what to say I should yell at him for cheating on me?" she asked.

"You never yelled at me. You just looked so…broken. Yelling would have been much better. Next time you can yell at me."

She shook her head. "No next time, Nick."

"You're right. Next time, I'll get it right and we'll be together forever."

"Why are you giving me advice when you're such a complete and total disaster?" she asked.

"Because it's much easier to see how to fix you than it is me," he explained.

Emily poked her head in the room. "What are you guys doing in here?"

"I was picking out her clothes," Nick said.

"Ah. Did you tell her to change her hair, too?"

"*Et tu,* roomie?" Jane asked, laying her hand protectively over her hair again.

"Change is good, Jane. Embrace it."

"I'll think about it. Maybe you guys can do pizza without me. I'm kind of zonked and tomorrow's a big day."

Emily and Nick made stilted eye contact. "You wanna?" Emily asked.

"Sure," Nick said. He rolled off the bed and poked Jane. "Schemer."

"Be nice," she said, blowing him a kiss.

"Be brave," he returned, and she made no reply.

CHAPTER 10

Blue knocked on Jane's door at six the next morning, and a man answered. "Oh," he exclaimed because he hadn't expected to see a man. "I'm looking for Jane."

"Yes," the man said. He seemed to be waging war with himself until at last he stepped aside and granted Blue access. "Come in, I'm Nick. That's Emily."

"Hi," Emily called. She sat at a tiny table drinking something out of a mug. There was another mug across from her and a selection of bagels. "Would you like coffee or a bagel?"

"I'm good, thanks," Blue said, adjusting the strap of his messenger bag. The rest of his luggage was waiting downstairs in the taxi.

"Janie, your ride's here," Nick called.

Jane poked her head out, eyed Blue, and emerged with her suitcase. "Good morning," she said, smiling.

"Good morning," Blue replied.

"Did you meet Emily, my roommate, and Nick, our friend and temporary couch mate until his apartment situation gets worked out."

"We met, thanks," Blue said.

"Okay. Goodbye," she said, turning to face her friends. To Blue's further surprise, they both stepped forward and hugged her tightly. The guy also kissed her cheek.

"Be safe, we love you, text to let us know you got there," Nick said.

"Will do," Jane agreed.

"Have fun," Emily added.

"But not too much," Nick said.

Jane made no reply. She wheeled her suitcase through the door and closed it behind them.

"Here, let me," Blue offered. He reached for her suitcase. Their hands brushed, and she did the thing where she jumped and jerked her hand away. Now that Blue knew why, he found it kind of flattering. And it was also making him hyper aware of those little touches, to the point where he was tempted to reach for her hand with his free one and hold it. Today she wore a light pink dress with some kind of print on it, horses on closer inspection, and it was the first time he'd ever seen her wearing anything other than black. The change brought more color to her cheeks, or maybe that was her embarrassment over jumping again when he touched her.

They reached the taxi downstairs. The cab driver tossed her suitcase in the trunk along with Blue's, and they were off.

"You seem especially close to your roommates."

"We go back a long way, since freshman year of college," Jane explained. "They're like family."

"How old are you?" he blurted. He was used to finding out everything about a person online. But Jane was a black hole, a blank. She had no online presence, and the lack was still driving him crazy. How was he supposed to learn anything about her? Outside of actually asking her, of course, but no one did that anymore.

"Twenty seven, almost twenty eight."

"How does someone so young already have her doctorate?" he asked.

"Because I was homeschooled. I graduated high school at sixteen, started college at seventeen, graduated at twenty, got my doctorate in four years, and have been at the museum for three. How did you get into computers?" she asked.

"I wasn't good at sports, and there's not a lot of space in the world for boys who can't toss a ball. I turned to video games, realized I had an affinity for all things binary, and the rest is history."

"How did you go from video games to prison?" she asked and the driver glanced at them in the rearview mirror.

"I got in with the wrong gang, an online gang of hackers who kept challenging me to do more and more things. Eventually I did the really wrong thing and got caught." He paused. "I still feel a lot of guilt for what I put my parents through. I'm not from a broken, messed up home or anything. I have loving parents. My mom's a teacher, my little brother is a golden child who has never done wrong. And then there's me."

"It would seem you've done a lot lately to make up for it. They must be proud of you."

"I hope so," he said. As much as he feared The Colonel and sometimes made fun of his over-the-top starched persona, he also owed him a debt of gratitude he could never repay. He had plucked him out of a life carrying the stigma of a convicted felon. Who besides the United States Government would have hired him with such a checkered past?

They made it through the airport check in line in a timely fashion. Blue was conscious of their surroundings, keeping an eye out in case they were being tailed. Jane seemed to have the same sort of mindfulness, and he found it odd. In his experience, not many civilians practiced situational awareness. Either Jane had been the victim of some sort of trauma that made her wary or she had been trained. But if she had been trained, by whom? And if she had been the victim of trauma, what sort? He had questions, but he didn't yet know her well enough to ask, and the lack of answers was pinging on his radar and making him suspicious. If only he could look into her online. Usually when he met a woman, he knew everything about her before the first date, down to kindergarten teacher and the name of her first pet. People put an immense amount of information online—health history, income, family details, personal anecdotes. Now he was flying blind, and it was making him crazy.

Why, for instance, was she suddenly so tense? She had seemed calm and relaxed for most of the morning, but now her face was drawn, her hands clenched. *Ask her, stupid.*

"Are you okay?" he asked.

"I'm fine but I'm going to get pulled out of line and searched," she said.

"Why? You're the least suspicious looking person I've ever seen." Unless the TSA knew something he didn't.

"I've been to a lot of countries with high terror alerts," she said. "Happens every time."

Sure enough, once they made their way forward, she was pulled aside and searched while Blue, with his sleeve tattoos and shockingly cerulean hair, was waved easily through.

"I feel like I just witnessed your honeymoon with that TSA agent," Blue said when she pulled on her sweater and rejoined him.

"Seriously. I'm going to start hiding small metal objects on my body to make it worth their while," she said, and he laughed. They boarded the plane.

"My friend is a huge fan of your work," she said once they were seated.

"My work?" he echoed.

"Your app. His grandma's neighbor is Martha Stewart's cousin."

"Ah, see that's why I did it, because otherwise the world wouldn't have that information."

"It's incredibly important," she said.

"Your life is richer for knowing it. You're welcome."

"Do you still invent apps?"

"I piddle, but nothing has come of it," he said.

"I wish there was an app for people with social anxiety. I'd be all over that," she said.

"Like what, for instance?"

"Like when your mind goes blank it would offer up a suggestion for what to say. Sort of like Google translate for awkward people."

"That's actually a really good idea," he said. "I might work on that, but rest assured I'll be sure to give you a cut of my royalties. How does ten dollars sound?"

She whistled. "I'm not comfortable with that kind of money. I'll waive my fee and find contentment that I've helped other people like me not say, 'You, too,' when a waitress says, 'Enjoy your meal.'"

"I'll put in an Easter egg of you macing someone," he said.

She covered her mouth and laughed. "My friend really liked your Easter egg in Threeple."

Too late she realized her mistake. "You put my name in? You were talking about me to your friend?"

"Is that the landing gear or is the plane breaking up?" she asked, turning to look out the window.

"Nice evasion," he said.

"I may have been talking about you a bit," she admitted.

"What did you say?" he asked.

"That you're highly professional in your capacity as my coworker," she said.

He leaned slightly closer. "I feel that you're lying, Dr. Dunbar."

She leaned closer and rested her hand on his forearm. "Prove it."

They were professionals on a crowded early morning business flight, but the temptation to kiss her was nearly irresistible. How had he gone from loathing to attraction in such a short span of time? Maybe the two emotions were closer together than they were farther apart.

"Pretzels?" the flight attendant asked and they both turned to look at her in confusion as if it were a foreign word, causing her to repeat it with slightly more irritation. "Pretzels."

"No, thanks," they each said, and she moved on.

"Until this moment, I never knew 'pretzels' could sound like a threat," Jane said.

"I kind of want coffee, but I'm afraid of what she'll do to it," Blue admitted.

"Ew, airplane coffee is atrocious. I know a good place on the way to the museum."

"How well do you know New York?" he asked.

"Like a second home. I did my undergrad there."

"Really?" Blue said. Everything about her was surprising because he had no foreknowledge of anything she was going to say. Usually when he was with a woman his biggest challenge was pretending he didn't already know what she was about to tell him. But with Jane he had no idea about anything.

"Yes. I moved there three weeks after my seventeenth birthday and lived there until I graduated. I love it."

"I've only been on business, and I never have time to explore," he said.

"Tonight, after we're finished at the museum, I could show you some places, if you want," she offered, suddenly finding something highly interesting on her cuticle.

"Yes," he agreed. He had to go with her regardless of what he wanted. Ridge had been clear on that. *You stick to her like double sided tape, no exceptions.* But he found he wanted to go, more because he was curious about where she might take him than because of any tourist spots he wanted to see. "I want. What did you have in mind?"

"What are you up for?"

"Anything," he said.

"Anything?" she asked.

"Anything," he said, and she smiled.

"Excellent, but now the pressure's on to find something good that will impress you."

"I'm actually very easily impressed. You know when you go to a place that has a clear elevator and you can see the mechanism that makes it go up and down? That keeps me enthralled for hours."

"I don't think I can top a clear elevator, but I'll try to come up with something," she said.

Their flight was only an hour. They arrived at the airport and hailed a taxi that would take them to their hotel and the museum, another hour. The cost would be exorbitant, but it was on the government's dime.

"I love the smell of New York," Jane whispered when they were safely tucked in the taxi.

"All I smell is man sweat," Blue whispered in reply.

"That and old fish and garbage is New York." She breathed deeply, smiling.

"I'm seeing a whole new side of you."

"And the day has only begun," she said. "See that building?" She ducked so he could see over her head, but it wasn't necessary since he was so much taller. "That was designed by Evan Falcone. He won a contest and I had a few classes with him when I was in school."

"What else can you show me? Give me the grand tour," Blue said.

"Are you sure that wouldn't be boring?"

"Again, extremely low threshold for what I consider boring, and I like knowing all the behind the scenes insider stuff."

"Okay, here we go." She took a breath and launched into an informative tour that lasted the entire drive. He had never heard her talk so much or so freely and he began to see what she must be like when she was in her natural element and at her best—intelligent, interesting, funny.

"Are you sure I'm not boring you?" she asked.

"Really, really not," he said.

"To be continued after work," she said.

"I'll be looking forward to it," he said, which might have been the understatement of the century.

CHAPTER 11

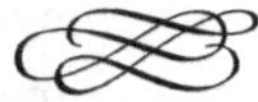

As before, the examination of the artifact took hours. Unlike before, Jane had only a professional rapport with her counterparts at this museum. While he waited for her, Blue did his homework on each person she met with, and the results were enlightening.

Dr. Andrew Stone, for instance, was on heavy doses of medication for depression and insomnia. He was also in the middle of a nasty divorce and had a history of gambling addiction. If anyone had motive to make extra cash, it was him. And he certainly had the knowledge, given that Blue only understood about every ten words he said, but the forgeries had taken time, effort, and energy. Dr. Stone seemed lacking in all three, given the massive doses of medication and lack of sleep.

Dr. Theresa Coleman had spent nearly a hundred thousand dollars on infertility treatments with no success. In addition to trying to conceive a child, she was in a near desperate search for a husband, if her ten cross postings on multiple dating sites were any indication. She also had a hundred thousand dollars in student loan debt and was facing eviction from her apartment. She had to be desperate for cash but, again, would she have the time and energy for intricate forgeries?

There were two lab assistants. Jerome Calder had a sealed juvenile record for vandalism but had been clean since then. Marjorie Tanner was clean as a whistle as far as the law went but, going five years back, Blue found some unsavory racially charged postings on an anti-government site and nothing since. Either she had changed her views or gone underground and learned to cover her tracks.

And then there was Jane Dunbar. Invisible Jane with no record of any kind. As if she felt his thoughts on her, she turned and smiled at him. In his current suspicious mood, the smile could have been chilling, but it wasn't. It was sweet and a tiny bit flirtatious. The combination kicked his heart into overdrive. *I like her,* Blue thought. If only he could quash the bit of lingering suspicion. Ten years of working in intelligence taught him everyone had skeletons. Sometimes, like him, they were early indiscretions, not indicative of lifelong character. Other times it was a slow boil, years of mistakes and broken laws culminating in a career of subversive behavior. He had never encountered anyone like Jane, a blank, a question mark. With no information, his mind was too busy filling in the blanks.

For lunch, the museum catered a meal. Blue found it interesting how easily everyone put up a façade—casual, happy, in control. In reality the assembled group had debt, infertility, mental illness, insomnia, and loneliness, among other things. Sometimes he felt like a voyeur, but it was his job to learn things about people, to dig into their pasts and find out what secrets they were trying to hide.

"Are you bored?" Jane whispered as lunch wore down and the museum's employees returned to work.

"As long as I have my computer, I'm never bored," Blue said. When he wasn't snooping into other people's lives, he sank into the virtual world, one of his own design.

"It's not looking good with the artifact," Jane continued in a whisper, leaning into him slightly. "I have a few more tests to run, but I suspect it's a fraud."

She was very close to his ear, leaning in to be better heard. He resisted the urge to tuck her hair behind her ear to better see her face, to touch her. "Is there anything I can do to help?" Blue offered, knowing the answer would be no. He was completely over his head in her world. He knew as much about ancient Egyptian relics as she did about coding and apps.

"Moral support. They're not going to take it well," Jane replied.

"I'm here for you," he assured her and then, because he couldn't resist anymore, reached out and pushed a lock of hair behind her ear. Her cheeks tinted faintly pink, and he smiled. When was the last time everything had clicked this way? When he had been attracted to a woman and she had felt the same? Jane was quieter, more conservative than his usual type. But she was also funny and intelligent, and he liked her, maybe a lot.

"I should probably get back to work," she said, dragging her eyes away from him.

"You could phone it in, fake the tests, and we could be out of here in ten minutes," he teased.

"Don't tempt me," she said so seriously he couldn't tell if she was joking.

When she returned to work, Blue attempted once again to locate her, this time switching to the dark web. He was about to give up when suddenly her name pinged out like a beacon. Unfortunately for him the rest of the page was encrypted and Blue's decryption key was on his home computer and not his laptop. His mind raced, wondering what the site said and how he could have missed it on his first search. Worse, it was a hacker's site. Why would hackers be talking about Jane?

Several hours later, she delivered her conclusion to the other scientists: the artifact was another fraud. Like before, it was an excellent, sophisticated forgery. As predicted, they were devastated. Blue didn't get it. To him it was a simple jade scarab. To them it represented much more, authenticity and provenance that had now been ruined.

They thanked their hosts and stepped outside into a bustling Manhattan weekday. "Where to, tour guide?" Blue asked.

"What are you up for?" Jane asked.

"Anything," Blue said.

"I'm going to hold you to that," she said and raised her hand for a taxi.

A half hour later they landed in Chinatown. Jane led them through crowded streets to a restaurant with no visible English written anywhere.

"What would you like?" she asked once they stepped inside.

"Um," he said, scanning the wall for a menu. Everything was in Mandarin. "I have no idea."

"Are you picky?"

"No."

"Do you trust me to order for you?" she said.

"Completely," he said and stepped back while she stepped forward to order in Mandarin. Jane retrieved chopsticks and sauce and they found a small table in the back.

"Exactly how many languages do you speak?" he asked. This morning she'd spoken Sanskrit while reading an object.

"The number changes depending on the fluency. I can speak a smattering from every place I've lived. We lived in China for six months when I was eleven. I learned enough to order food and read a few signs."

"What did you order?" he asked.

"It's a surprise." She opened her chopsticks and laid them on a napkin.

"This is the point where I confess to you I have never been able to master chopsticks," he said.

"I'll show you how a friend in China showed me." She placed the chopsticks between his thumb and third finger. "Grip it as if you're holding a pencil. Now lay the other one on top and rest your index finger gently on top of it."

"That's a lot easier, but I'm still fairly certain I'm going to end up wearing most of my meal."

"I promise not to notice if you're covered in food."

Their food arrived a few minutes later. Jane had ordered an assortment of dumplings and dim sum as well as fresh squid.

"This one's my favorite, but be careful because it has hot soup in it," Jane warned.

"There's hot soup in the dumpling?"

"Yes, and it's amazing."

"How does one eat it?"

She demonstrated, using her chopsticks.

"You make it look so easy," he said. He attempted to take a dumpling and failed miserably.

"I think I have something that can help, if you like," Jane said.

"A fork?" he asked hopefully. He hadn't been able to find any so far.

"No, a rubber band." She dug in her purse, pulled one out, and wound it around the top of his chopsticks. Then she rolled a piece of paper and stuck it between the two sticks. "Leverage."

He tested the new arrangement, easily pinching the sticks. "This is so much better. Why doesn't everyone do this?"

"A lot of small children do," she said, and he laughed.

A half hour later, they stumbled out, their bellies stuffed. "That was amazing. I'm never going to be able to eat at a so-called Chinese buffet again," Blue said.

"I'm glad you enjoyed it," she said.

"I really did," he assured her. "What else do you have planned for me?"

"A few things, but I've been having second thoughts. These are things I enjoyed when I was here, but I was seventeen, unable to go to clubs or bars or anywhere exciting or illicit. I don't want to bore you."

"Jane, I'm twenty nine. I haven't been to a club in seven years. On my last day off I spent eight hours in an online gaming tournament. Please believe me when I tell you my life is far less interesting or exciting than whatever you're imagining. I want to see the city through your eyes. A day in the life of Jane, or rather an evening in the life."

"Okay, let's go." She tossed her hand in the air, hailed a taxi, and gave him the address. Twenty minutes later, they arrived in front of a building Blue didn't recognize. Jane flashed an ID, and they were admitted entrance.

"What is this place?" Blue asked.

"The Explorers Club," Jane replied. "My dad is a member and used to take me here whenever we were in New York. I thought it was the coolest place ever as a kid. When I moved here, I joined and used to hang out whenever I was homesick and missing him."

"I had no idea this existed," Blue said. It was a literal explorer's club, founded by some of the people who first trekked to the Arctic and discovered unmapped territories. The space was filled with exploits, taxidermy animals, and incredible souvenirs, and the building itself was spectacular. Jane led him on a quick tour, giving him the highlights of what could have lasted days, given the amount of things to see.

She checked her phone for the time. "Ready?"

He wasn't; he could stay for hours more, inspecting all the cool sights at the club. But now he was curious to see what else she had planned. "Ready," he agreed. This time they walked to their destination, a few blocks and then Jane took his arm.

"Here," she said. He looked around, but it appeared like any boring street corner.

"No, *here*." She pointed to the ground. Blue looked down and saw a section of rock enclosed in glass.

"What is it?"

"It's the Portal Down to Old New York. In 1975, they did an archaeological dig and located the remains of the first Dutch colony from the 1640's. This is it. We're standing where settlers stood four hundred years ago."

"This is so unbelievably cool," Blue breathed, crouching to get a better look. "I had no idea they did an archaeological dig in the middle of Manhattan."

"Most people walk over it every day with no idea," Jane said. "It always felt like my little secret, kind of. My connection with all the people who have come through New York for the last four hundred years."

Blue pulled out his phone and took a picture and then took a selfie before pulling Jane alongside and taking one of her, too.

"I'd ask you to tag me in that, but basically you'd have to pin it to a literal bulletin board and write my name on it," she joked.

He wanted to ask her about her lack of online presence and social media, but he sensed the topic was deeper and more taboo than he wanted to approach. The night was fun and interesting, and he didn't want to do anything to spoil it. She checked the time on her phone.

"We have to hurry," she said and jetted away so quickly he had to jog to keep up with her.

The next place they went was somewhere he recognized, but he wasn't sure what they were doing there. Jane led him into Grand Central Station and positioned him against a wall.

"Stay right here. Don't move," she ordered. He watched as she walked across the massive room. He had no idea what she was doing, and then he heard it, a tiny whisper. It had to be some kind of fluke or anomaly to hear her small voice above the din of the teeming crowd of people.

"If you can hear me, turn toward the wall and whisper," Jane murmured.

"How are you doing this?" he whispered to his wall.

"The miracle of architecture," she whispered in reply.

He turned to face her again and saw her smiling and beckoning to him. He went forward, and she checked the time again. "It's almost sundown. Are you ready?"

"For what?"

"Rest," she said before turning to walk away from him again.

Blue trotted behind eagerly this time, curious to see where she would choose next. They wended their way through busy Manhattan streets and intersections, finally landing at a nearly hidden escalator in the middle of the sidewalk. They ascended the escalator, and Blue nearly gasped with shock and delight. At the top of the escalator was a paradise, a lush garden, so still and quiet it felt like an oasis. They selected a bench and watched the sun sink over the city, not speaking, merely enjoying the quiet beauty of the evening.

"This evening has been…" he couldn't think of the word he wanted to say. Exciting? It hadn't been. They hadn't done much of anything, but it had been interesting and…restorative, maybe? They had connected with the past in a way he hadn't imagined, first through the world's bravest explorers and then the archaeological site and the architectural secret. And then they lost themselves in nature, in the middle of Manhattan. All in all, Jane Dunbar had taken Blue completely by surprise, and he loved it. It was like opening a cardboard box with no anticipation, only to reveal your dream present inside. She looked ordinary and unassuming, but Jane Dunbar was cool, probably way cooler than him, and he was at a bit of a loss as to know what to do with her.

"Did you think it was over?" Jane asked, smiling.

"It's not?" he asked, his heart beating hard. They were isolated in the park, sheltered by a tree and the half-moonlight. She sat close beside him on the bench and, once again, he reached out and pushed her hair behind her ear, itching for more, wanting to touch her, to kiss her again.

"Everything so far has been something I enjoy. But you're a gamer, so I thought we could do something for you," she said.

"Internet café?" he guessed, unable to imagine what she might think would be for him.

"You'll see," she said. She did the thing where she stood up and began walking away again, beckoning him to follow without saying a word or lifting a finger. It was as if she had him on some kind of invisible tether, and he couldn't *not* go with her.

They took a taxi again and stopped in front of an unassuming little building on a nothing side street. Blue got out and inspected the sign.

"It's a Laundromat," he announced. "This is what you think I enjoy?" He was only half joking. Unless it was some kind of speakeasy, he couldn't imagine what might be inside that would hold his interest.

"You'll see," she repeated, stepping aside to allow him access. They took a few steps in, the scent of detergent and fabric softener rushing forth to greet them. Blue looked at Jane in question. She took his hand and began weaving through machines until they spilled into a back room filled to the brim with every conceivable pinball machine.

"Pinball," he said stupidly.

"Pinball," Jane agreed. "I have to warn you I spent so much time here when I was a kid that I got pretty good. No, I'm being modest. I'm kind of amazing."

"I'm going to need you to prove it," Blue said, withdrawing a ten from his wallet.

"One request: please don't cry when I beat you," Jane said.

"Care to make a little wager, doctor?" he asked.

"How much did you have in mind?" she said.

"If I win, you have to tell me why you have no virtual footprint, why you're so off the grid."

"Deal," she said. "And if I win, you have to show me a picture of you from middle school."

He groaned. "How did you know that would be my Achilles heel?"

"Lucky guess," she said.

"Now I definitely have to win. There's no coming back from my seventh grade school picture," he said.

Jane hadn't been exaggerating. The competition was fierce, lasting ninety minutes, until after midnight. In the end, she won.

"How does an anthropologist have such good hand/eye coordination?" he asked.

"Lots of dusting things with tiny brushes," Jane said and, despite her best intentions, fought a yawn.

"I guess that's a wrap," Blue said.

"I have to confess I have no idea what happens in this city after midnight. I always had morning classes and conked out early," Jane said. "It's ten blocks back to our hotel. Walk or taxi?"

He stared down at her, wanting to do whatever was possible to prolong the mood of the evening. "Walk."

They turned and headed in the direction of their hotel. In true New York fashion, the streets were still filled with people. A few times they had to squeeze together to avoid bumping into someone. Their hands brushed, and Blue took hers, letting his fingers wind their way through hers.

They reached the hotel and he held the door for her. The walk to the elevator and their rooms was quiet, expectant. They stopped outside of Jane's room and faced each other.

"Thank you for such an amazing and interesting evening," Blue said. "It was fun." He still held her hand. He brought it to his chest, clutching it between both his hands now.

"Thank you, I had fun, too." An awkward lull fell between them. Jane glanced at her door. "Would you like to come in for a cup of monumentally bad hotel room coffee?"

Blue looked at the door, too. "Thanks, but it's been a long day, and I'm kind of exhausted."

"Oh. Good night then."

"Good night, Jane." He let go of her hand and waited until she was safely inside before going to his room.

CHAPTER 12

Jane leaned on the door a minute and pulled her phone from her pocket.

Weird day, she texted Emily who worked second shift at the mental hospital and was probably now riding the Metro home.

How so? By the way, you're right, he's super cute. Like a blue-haired Keanu Reeves. I thought Nick might bust a neck artery after you guys left.

We had a good day and an even better evening. It felt more like a date than a business arrangement. He walked me to my door, mostly because his door is right next to it. And that was it.

No kiss? Emily asked.

Nothing. I invited him inside. He said no.

Ouch, that's not good. She added a crying emoji.

I guess I misread him, and he's not interested, Jane typed.

Maybe he's really professional and serious about the job, Emily suggested.

He has blue hair and jokes all the time. It's not him, it's me. I'm man repellent, Jane said.

Uh, you had the same boyfriend for a decade, and he's still pining.

The mention of Nick made Jane remember what he'd told her. *I know about you two,* she typed.

What about us? Emily asked.

That you've been kissing.

WHAT?? Emily replied. *I'd ask if you're crazy, but I'm not supposed to say that word to my patients.*

Nick told me, Jane replied, squinting. Had he told her that, or had he merely failed to correct her assumption when she said it? The memory was hazy. Either way, why would he have been dishonest? Except Nick often tried to manipulate events for his own selfish purposes.

He was clearly having one over on you. I would never. Ew. He's like my brother and, hello, I saw him cheat on you three times. I'm not that dense, no offense.

None taken, Jane assured her.

My stop is coming up and I have to jet. I'm sorry it's not working out with Blue Keanu Reeves. His loss. Men are stupid.

Thanks, Jane replied, tucking her phone onto the nightstand. She wasn't yet ready for Emily's commiseration. Some men were stupid, but Blue wasn't. She liked him, but apparently the feeling wasn't mutual.

She readied herself for bed, lay down, and reached for the lamp when a soft knock sounded on the door. She sat up, wondering if her ears had deceived her. Another knock followed. She padded to the door and cracked it open. Blue stood on the other side.

"I have a problem," he blurted,

Jane opened the door wider. "What's that?"

"I say no when I mean yes."

"That's a big problem," Jane agreed.

"Practically a disability. It's cost me money, jobs, fame, and tonight it cost me the chance to spend a few extra minutes with this woman I had an amazing evening with."

"Yikes," Jane said. "Well, good night." She started to close the door, but he put his hand on it, pressing it back.

"Maybe you could help me try to overcome my malady," Blue suggested.

Jane paused. "Maybe, but only because you said malady. I'm a sucker for good vocabulary. What can I do?"

"You could try asking me to come in again," he said.

"With the coffee this time?" she asked.

"Skip the coffee," he said.

"Would you like to come in for a bit?"

"So much yes," he said, stepping inside and bending to kiss her in one swift motion. Jane stood on her toes and slid her arms around his neck, completely forgetting she was now in her pajamas. The door clicked softly closed behind him, and he took another step into the room, maintaining his hold on her.

They were in a hotel room, far from home, and the kiss began to reflect that, growing and morphing into dangerous territory in seconds. Jane's phone rang and, after a few beats, she put a hand on his chest and took a step back.

"I have to get that, hold on." She dashed for the bed, dropped the phone, and ran into the nightstand on her way to pick it up. "Ouch, hello. Yes, Dad, I'm fine. I hit my head on the nightstand. Just being clumsy, you know me. No, it's not too late. No, I was still up. Yes, I know I should probably be asleep. How are you? How's Mom? Mm, hmm. Mm, hmm. Good. Right. I know, I will. I love you, too." She was now perched on the edge of the bed. She pushed the button to end the call and set the phone back on the nightstand.

Blue stood a few feet away watching her with no small amount of satisfaction. She looked ruffled and flustered, her usually perfect hair slightly askew, her lips raw and red from his kisses. "That was your dad?" he asked.

"Yes. He only calls every few days to check in, but if I don't answer, he kind of freaks out. Sorry to cut off in the middle of," she motioned between them, "you know."

"It's okay." He sank onto the bed beside her, a safe six inches away. "It was probably for the best. Things seemed to be spiraling out of control."

"Definitely," she agreed.

"I should probably go," he said.

"That's probably for the best. Can I say one thing before you leave?"

"What's that?" he asked.

She bridged the distance between them and pressed her lips to his neck. He drew in a breath. "You make a good point with that," he said, his voice shaky. "Do I have time for a rebuttal?"

"Take all the time you need," she said.

He reached for her, pulling her close so he could kiss her again. Her arms snaked around his neck again, and she sat up on her knees to reach him better until they both eventually sank back onto the bed, side by side.

"Blue," she whispered, the pads of her fingers lightly touching his lips.

"What?" he whispered in return, his fingers stroking the side of her face.

"Nothing, I wanted to say your name."

"That's the first time you've ever said it," he said.

"I know."

"Why?"

"Because I was afraid it would come out all breathless and shaky," she said.

"I like you breathless and shaky," he said.

"That's how I feel all the time when I'm with you," she replied. He advanced, rolled her onto her back, and kissed her for a minute before she paused to speak again.

"I'm sorry," she whispered.

"For what?" he asked, smiling. Then he felt a sting on his neck, kind of like a bug bite. He turned to look and saw two men wearing masks and everything faded to black.

CHAPTER 13

Blue woke disoriented and groggy. What had happened to him? Something…something strange and bad, but what? Something about Jane. He couldn't quite grasp it at first, but his heart hammered hard with anxiety as he tried to remember.

The room around him was dark. His head was on something soft and good smelling. He tried to touch it with his fingers and realized his hands were bound behind his back.

"Are you awake?" It was Jane. She was the soft, delightfully scented thing beneath him. The thought brought him no pleasure, only fear, but why? *I'm sorry.* Her words floated back to him from the same moment the men drugged him. She had done this, she had tricked him, trapped him. He jerked away from her as fast and as far as possible, until he butted into the wall behind him.

"It's okay," Jane said in a soothing voice. She reached out a hand, feeling for him, honking his nose by mistake. "You're safe, you're all right. Everything is fine."

"Don't touch me," he hissed. Her fingers froze. He turned his head away from her grasp, and she withdrew her hand.

"Are you all right?" she whispered.

"Am I all right? Of course I'm not all right. Are you insane? Where are we?"

"I think somewhere on the wharf. I smell fish and kind of hear the water," Jane said.

"Who took us?" he growled, not because he meant to but because his voice was heavy with sleep and sedation. He cleared it, wishing for water.

"I have no idea," she said.

"Drop it, Jane. You don't have to pretend anymore."

There was a pause, and then she spoke again. "Pretend about what?"

"Is Jane even your real name?" he asked.

"What are you talking about? What did they give you? Are you having some kind of memory problem?"

She sounded almost convincingly alarmed. He laughed humorlessly. "No, I remember everything. I remember you saying you were sorry and then the men showed up. What was that phone call, really? Was it the signal for them to come get me? You pretend to call your dad and say a series of things to let them know you had me where you wanted me?"

"Huh?" she said.

"Stop, okay, stop pretending. Be honest about this whole thing. You set it all up, and you're the forger."

"Seriously, what?" she said. He could hear her shifting, and he braced himself in case she touched him again. He didn't think he could stand it, not after he had almost fallen for her, not after she had kissed him so freely, had urged him to believe they had a chance at something real. "You think I'm the forger? Why?"

"Because it all makes sense," he said.

"None of it makes sense. Why would I work with you?"

"To deflect attention," he said.

"Why would I say they were forgeries? Why wouldn't I authenticate my own work?"

"In case we get a second opinion."

"Let me get this straight—you think I'm not only a forger, but a talented criminal mastermind who somehow lured you into my web, made out with you, and kidnapped you in the middle of it? Riddle me this, Columbo, why did I kidnap myself?"

That gave him pause. "To get information out of me," he said triumphantly.

"So the last ninety minutes of cradling your unconscious form on top of me until my arms went numb and useless, that's all part of my master plan to interrogate you. Wow, I'm really good. I have to say, I'm impressed by me. I didn't think I had it in me."

He squinted, beginning to doubt the validity of his thought processes. He had been suspicious of her from the beginning. She had fed those suspicions with a few little things she'd said, but mostly with her complete lack of virtual footprint, something he found too odd to accept. "You apologized, and then the men took me. There's no way out of that one."

"Except there completely is," she said, and now she sounded irked.

"What?"

"I'm not telling," she said.

"Why would you not? Because it's a lie?"

"No, because it's embarrassing and you don't deserve to hear it," she said.

"You might as well tell me," he said. What else did they have to do alone in the darkness of wherever they were?

She was silent for so long he didn't think she would continue, but eventually she did. "I was trying to say I was sorry for spraying you in that elevator. I was going to say I wish I had kissed you instead. But then I saw the men. They knocked you out, apparently before you heard my screams. They gagged me and loaded us into the trunk of a car. You were unconscious; I was not. You were bound; I was not. I screamed and fought them, but there are two of them, and I weigh a hundred pounds. And they told me if I didn't stop fighting them, they would kill you, that it was me they were after, and you were expendable. So I stopped fighting, and here we are."

Oh. Uh-oh. It seemed he had made a huge mistake, but he only had her word for it. For all he knew, people could be in the room with them right now, watching through night vision goggles, waiting for him to crack, to confess. He was in possession of a mountain of secrets, missile sites, codes, online security, hacks he had personally perpetrated on other countries, on other world leaders, viruses he had created and distributed to take down entire networks of known enemies. In terms of sensitive information, he was a treasure trove. Was he really supposed to believe this was all about Jane? That she was the intended target of the kidnapping?

"What's in your pockets?" she asked.

"What?" His brain was still sluggish from whatever they'd given him, his tongue thick and furry with it.

Jane sighed, her annoyance with him in every molecule of carbon dioxide expelled from her body. "Did you empty your pockets before you came to my room, or is there anything in them that can help us?"

"See, it's things like that that make me suspicious," he said. "We've supposedly been kidnapped, and you're a civilian. Why aren't you in freakout panic mode? Why are you the one thinking of ways to get us out?"

"Because someone has to do it, and you seem unwilling or unable."

Ouch. She had a point, though. Technically, he was a trained agent. But outside of mandatory training, he had never been tested, never been put in a situation where he had to use his training. He could load, shoot, and clean a gun, but he did it twice a year to qualify. He had memorized the basics of self-defense, but he'd never been in a compromising position where he needed to use them. And now that he was, an anthropologist was the one concocting a plan to get them out.

"I still have stuff in my pockets. There's a flashlight on my keychain, on the right side."

She reached for him, feeling around until she located him, but couldn't get her hand inside his pocket. "Lie flat," she directed. He lay down. She tried contorting her hand, but the angle was wrong, Eventually she had to lay on him in order to slip her fingers into his jeans to reach the keys.

Blue closed his eyes, breathing through his mouth. Why did she have to smell so good and feel so soft against his chest? Either she was a terrorist and couldn't be trusted or she wasn't, and he had ruined things with her forever. It was a lose-lose situation.

"Stop enjoying this," Jane said, pushing against him to sit up again, keys in hand.

"Can't help it," he croaked. "You smell really good, and you're wearing silk pajamas."

"That's the required dress code for all the terrorists in my cell," she said, her tone dripping sarcasm. She located the flashlight on his keychain and shined it around the blackened interior where they were being kept. It was a large, cavernous space, far bigger than the reach of the flashlight. They were on a mattress on the floor, next to a wall. Across the room eyes peered at them, but they weren't the eyes of people. For one thing they were too low to the ground, and for another they gleamed golden in the flashlight's beam. *Rats.* Jane shuddered. She had spent years living in countries where rats were more than a nuisance; they were a danger. They had to get out of this place before the rats discovered them and came closer for a taste.

"Can you stand?" she asked.

"I won't know until I try," Blue said. "Hold on a sec." He wriggled his bound hands around his legs, bringing them to the front. It wasn't as good as being untied, but it was better. Somehow he knew that if Ridge or Ethan were in this position, they would already be out of the ropes and in charge of the scene. They would likely break their thumbs to get out of the bindings or some other super spy nonsense. Blue wasn't willing to go to those lengths to prove his masculinity, but he did want to have his hands available in case he needed them. Tentatively, he scooted off the bed and wobbled to a standing position.

Jane stood beside him, cocking her head to listen. "The water sounds like it's behind us, meaning we should go the opposite direction."

"Right," Blue agreed, though he hadn't given it a thought. He felt confused, disoriented, unable to focus. He hoped it was because of the drugging and not because he was inherently bad at this aspect of being an agent. Jane, on the other hand, was taking charge as if she were the female Jack Reacher. *Or like a spy who's had training.* He pushed that thought aside. Following her was better than remaining on the mattress and, for the moment, she seemed to be on the level and trying to get them out.

"I'm going to hold on to you so we don't get separated in the darkness. This is merely a precaution and not some terrorist tactic to try and overtake you," Jane warned, grasping his forearm.

"Should I expect everything you say from now on to be tinged with anger and sarcasm?" he asked.

"Absolutely," she replied.

Their progress was slow in the darkened warehouse. The space was massive so that even the addition of the tiny flashlight did nothing to help. And they had no idea what might be waiting in the darkness. It seemed likely that if someone was there, they would have sprung at them by now. But it was still an insecure feeling, not knowing what might lie a few feet in front of their faces. The sounds of water lapping outside and tiny feet scurrying inside did nothing to ease their anxiety.

Eventually they proceeded far enough to the opposite side of the warehouse that they saw a tiny speck of pale moonlight eking through a hole leading to the outside.

"There must be a door on this wall somewhere," Jane reasoned. She was still holding on to Blue with her left hand. With her right, she scanned the wall of the warehouse up and down as they moved forward. When her light glinted on something metal, she knelt and picked up an old screwdriver, adding it to her right hand along with the light.

After about twenty feet of walking, they reached a door and tried the handle. It turned but had been bolted shut from the outside.

"Stand back, I'll kick it," Blue said, feigning more bravado than he felt. Could he kick down a door? He had never tried, but he had the sense he probably should at least attempt it.

Jane had other ideas. "How about if I take it off the hinges instead," she said, using the found screwdriver to pop the pins free from the hinges.

"That's one way to go," Blue said. He stood uselessly by while she worked.

"Now kick it," she instructed. He did so, and the door popped easily free, the sound echoing loudly in the darkness of the wharf. They waited a while, hearts hammering, to see if anyone would come to check, but they had seemingly been deposited on their own to wait for who knew what.

Outside a light breeze was blowing, but it did nothing to dispel the smell of rotting fish. "It wasn't a long drive," Jane whispered. "We're somewhere in the vicinity of the city, possibly New Jersey." She scanned the area, and so did Blue. The moon was a sliver, not adding much light. And wherever they were wasn't well lit, as if begging for illegal and nefarious activities to take place.

They walked for what seemed like a very long time, until the wharf was far behind them and a neighborhood loomed up ahead. Blue tried to think of a plan. They would need to find a pay phone, if such a thing still existed anymore. He would call Ridge and have a contact from New York come get them. Or maybe Ridge would prefer to involve the police, given the precarious nature of their current situation. Blue's hands were still tied, they were both barefoot, and their kidnappers could come looking for them at any moment.

Jane began peering into car windows.

"What are you looking for?" Blue asked.

"An old car, something before computer chips," she said.

"Why?" he asked, but she didn't answer.

Eventually they landed beside an old Toyota. "Now what?" Blue asked. Jane didn't reply. Instead she began to shimmy out of her pajama shorts.

CHAPTER 14

"Why are you getting naked?" Blue exclaimed, staring at her with a combination of dismay and fascination.

Jane didn't answer. Instead she picked up a large rock, palmed it, wrapped her shorts around the rock and her hand, and shattered the back window of the car.

"What are you doing?" Blue hissed, his frantic gaze skirting the horizon. Certainly someone had noticed a half dressed woman bashing in a car's window. But no. No one turned on a light, poked a head out a window, or showed up to arrest her.

Jane opened the driver side door, shook the glass out of her shorts, and put them back on. "Get in if you're coming," she said before slipping behind the wheel.

Blue scurried around to the passenger side, struggled the door open, and eased inside. "What, are you planning to hotwire this thing?"

"Of course not," Jane said. She took the pilfered screwdriver, stuck it into the ignition, and used the rock like a hammer to bang it into place. Satisfied, she tossed the rock outside, closed the door, and turned the screwdriver. The car roared to life. She put it into gear and took off, all while Blue stared at her, shocked and speechless.

"What the actual world, Jane?" he declared at last.

She didn't reply.

"You can't drive," he added.

"Who says?" she replied.

"You! You don't have a license."

"I said I didn't have a license, not that I couldn't drive. Who can't drive a car? What am I, Amish?"

"I don't know, Jane, do Amish people take off their pants and steal cars?" he said. Not only was she driving, but it was a standard transmission, something Blue had no idea how to use. And she was doing ninety on the freeway. Belatedly, he fumbled for his seatbelt. It was hard to buckle it one handed. Jane reached across him to help.

"Both hands on the wheel," he snapped, but she ignored him and clicked his belt closed.

"In case we get pulled over. The fines on no belt are huge," she said.

Was she joking? She was driving a stolen car, one stolen by her, and she was worried about a ticket? "Prison is not going to go well for you," he mumbled.

She snorted a laugh but otherwise ignored him.

They sped out of the city. Blue wasn't a genius with directions, but he was certain they were going the wrong way.

"Where are you taking us?" he asked.

"To my criminal lair. We'll see what the Kingpin wants to do with you," she said, not bothering to look at him.

"Jane," he pressed, but she said nothing else until eventually even he recognized where they were. "The airport? You can't go to the airport."

"Pretty sure I can," Jane said.

"You have no ticket, no money, no ID, no shoes, *no bra*."

"I'll alert Anna Wintour at *Vogue* I'm dressed all wrong for a heist and flight."

"Okay, you're mad, I get that, but you can't stroll up to an airplane and say 'fly me to DC' without the things I mentioned."

She skidded to a halt in front of the drop off gate, used a napkin from the floor to wipe down her half of the car and tossed it at him.

"Watch me. Wipe down your side unless you want to go back to prison. Your prints are definitely on file." Then she opened the door, got out, and disappeared.

Blue sat in the car for a solid two minutes, positive Jane would return, possibly in handcuffs. When she didn't, he struggled out of the car, remembered he needed to wipe it down, and returned to the car. After wiping it clean of his prints, he sprinted inside, barefoot, his hands still tied in front of him.

Maybe they had detained Jane on entry. He imagined himself trying to explain to airport security. *You see, officers, she's apparently had some type of mental break that turned her from a mild-mannered anthropologist to one of the hookers from* Grand Theft Auto. But when he walked inside, she wasn't detained by one of the guards. In fact, she was nowhere in sight. As usual, JFK teemed with masses of people, too many to find one tiny doctor, even if she was barefoot and wearing silky pajamas.

As before, Blue had no idea what to do. Should he try to hail a taxi —barefoot and bound—make it back to the hotel, and call Ridge? Or should he look for a phone here and call his boss? He imagined trying to find someone at JFK that would believe him. It would take forever. They would detain him and probably call Ridge for him. He would rather be the one to tell the story, knowing already it was going to be humiliating and might possibly get him in a heap of trouble. The one thing Ridge had asked him to do, *the one thing,* was to keep an eye on Jane, to keep her safe.

He walked back outside. Security was already surrounding the car he'd arrived in. As nonchalantly as possible, he bypassed them, walked up to a cab, opened the door, and slid inside. "Hotel Manafort in Manhattan," he said.

The driver took off, and Blue breathed a sigh of relief. Now he only had to hope his ID and phone were still in his room back at the hotel. Had whoever nabbed him also taken his things? He'd know in an hour.

"Wait here, my wallet is inside," Blue said when they finally arrived back at the hotel. The cabbie turned to scowl at him.

"No way, buddy, I've heard that one before."

Blue showed him his rope-bound hands. "Do I look like I can make an easy escape? It's been a rough night. Just give me a couple of minutes, and I'll throw in an extra twenty."

"You got five minutes," the cab driver said.

Blue hopped out, sprinted to the elevator, ran to his room, worked the key out of his pocket, opened the door and, to his great relief, saw his wallet and phone sitting where he'd left them. Had it only been a few hours ago that he had set them on his nightstand to go see Jane, full of hope and promise and romance?

Not pursuing that line of thought further, he took his wallet back downstairs and paid the cabbie. "I don't suppose you have a knife in there that could cut me loose," Blue said.

The cabbie reached under the seat, pulled out an eight-inch blade, sliced through Blue's ropes, and took off. He seemed so unfazed Blue wondered if it wasn't the first night he'd had to cut a rider free.

Blue turned back toward the hotel, palming his phone. He was out of excuses and time; he'd have to call Ridge. He hit the button on his phone.

"What's the bad news, Blue?" Ridge greeted him.

"How do you know it's bad news?" Blue replied.

"I have a sense about these things," Ridge said. "How's Jane?"

"She was fine the last time I saw her."

There was a pause. "The last time you saw her? Explain quickly before I reach through the phone and rip out your tonsils."

"My tonsils have already been removed."

"Then I'll find some new ones and paste them on you. Quit stalling."

"We got taken."

"Okay, I'm going to go ahead and assume that either you got free again or your kidnappers have a liberal cell phone policy," Ridge said.

"We got free."

"Who took you?"

"No idea. They knocked me out. Before that I saw black masks. I don't think Jane saw them either, but you'd have to ask her. They talked to her, so maybe she heard something identifiable."

"Get to the part where you lost her," Ridge urged.

"I didn't lose her; she lost me. Rather, she left me bound and barefoot at the airport after she stole a car like friggin' MacGyver."

There was silence on the phone so long, Blue thought Ridge had hung up. Then he heard Maggie's voice. "Hello?"

"Hello."

"Blue, what did you say to Ridge? I've never seen him laugh so hard."

"Nothing."

"Tell me."

"No. You'll end up the same way."

"I don't think that's possible. He's about to rupture something internal. Can you crack an appendix from laughing?"

"Promise you won't laugh," he said.

"I'll try," Maggie said.

Blue took a breath. "Jane stole a car and left me barefoot and bound at the airport."

It took a second. He could practically picture her trying to push back the laughter, but of course she didn't succeed. She erupted like Mt. St. Helen's. "Pfffft," was all he heard as she sputtered and dropped the phone.

"Good talk," he yelled. "I can always count on you two for support." He ended the call, Ridge and Maggie's laughter ringing in the background. He had barely enough time to shower, pack his things, grab a cup of coffee and a pastry, and hail yet another taxi back to the airport. It was a good thing the trip was for work or he would have to take out a small loan for taxi fare. He was up to almost four hundred dollars now and counting.

The airport was as busy as it had been a few hours ago, if not more. Blue made it through security with no problems again and boarded his plane on time. He sat and stared at the empty seat beside him, expectantly waiting for Jane to arrive. When she didn't, he felt antsy and anxious, wondering what had become of her. For the first time in a few hours, he had a chance to reflect on the events of the past day and night.

What if Jane *had* staged the kidnapping? That would certainly explain how she got them out of it with such ease, and also why she had disappeared after. But if she was the forger, what had been her motivation for the kidnapping? And why was Blue seemingly the only person who found her suspicious? And how was it possible he was both equal parts distrustful of and attracted to her?

Wherever she was, he hoped she was okay.

CHAPTER 15

Back in DC, Jane let herself into her apartment and leaned on the door, sighing with exhaustion and too many other emotions to name. She plopped onto the couch, not bothering to shed her borrowed finery.

Nick emerged from the back and jumped in surprise at the sight of her. "I thought you weren't due home for hours."

"Change of plans," she murmured.

"What are you wearing?" he asked.

"Clothes from the airport lost and found."

"Why?"

"Long story," Jane said.

"I didn't think you'd be home for a while. I was working on an art project in your room, but I can move it," he turned helplessly toward her room.

"It's fine, leave it," Jane said, her tone listless.

"Are you okay?" he asked.

"Yes," she said and promptly burst into tears.

Nick, who was used to Jane's tendency toward easy tears, wasn't alarmed. He sat beside her on the couch. "Are these sad tears, angry tears, or exhausted tears?"

"Everything tears," she said.

"I take it things with the guy did not go well," he said.

"Things did not go well," she said, scrubbing her eyes. "And I had to call in a favor from one of my dad's contacts to get home."

"Have you ever had to call in a favor before?" he asked.

"No," she wailed, miserable. She had tried so hard to survive on her own over the years, never depending on her dad's name or reputation for anything. And now at the age of twenty seven, she'd been forced to regress to a childlike dependency on that which she had eschewed for so long.

"I'm sorry," Nick said, pulling her close for a hug.

"No you're not," Jane murmured.

"No I'm not," he agreed. "It killed me to see you go off with him, knowing you might end up liking him more than me. And it makes me incredibly gleeful to see how miserably he's failed you. I bet I'm looking pretty good now, in comparison."

She raised her head to glare at him.

"Or possibly not." He pulled her into his lap, and she rested her head on his shoulder. His hand rubbed her back in a soothing circle. He was safe and familiar, and Jane began to relax. And then he tried to kiss her.

Jane put up her hand, pushing him away. "Nick, no."

"Come on, Jane. Look, you tried it with someone else, and it didn't work out. I think that's because you're still in love with me."

She laughed a little, sniffing. "I'm sure you do."

"It's been a while since we gave it a go. Let's try us again. We can make it this time, I know it."

"And when some other woman comes along you believe might be your true soul mate, what happens to me then?" she asked.

He shook his head. "I've tried it three times with other women, and it never works. I always come back to you."

"This is the crux of the problem between us, Nick. You think the coming back should please me, but it's the going away in the first place that destroys me. Last time you swore, you *swore*, you wouldn't cheat on me again. You said we'd get back together, get things smoothed out, and get married. And instead I walked in on you with another woman because you're not even good at hiding it."

"I'm good at hiding," he said, offended.

"Really, incredibly not helping. The point is that you've been a big part of my life since I was seventeen years old, and I love you for that. You'll always have that sweet spot in my heart, my first love. And you miraculously remain one of my best friends. But in the immortal words of the great philosopher Taylor Swift, we are never, ever, ever getting back together."

"We'll see," Nick replied undaunted.

Jane groaned. He rubbed her back again. "Do you want to tell me about it?"

"No. I'm exhausted, I want to sleep. Is your art project on my bed?"

"No."

"Good, then I'll sleep in there."

"Go, but Jane, when you wake up, we need to have another conversation," he said, his tone serious.

"'Kay," she murmured, easing past him to slip into her room. It smelled like paint and something she couldn't identify, but she didn't care. She crawled into bed, curled into a ball, and fell promptly asleep.

When she woke several hours later, her head felt clearer, her heart lighter. The reality was that she never had to see Blue again. Her work with him and his team was voluntary. She would simply call Ridge and tell him she couldn't continue. She would give him the name of a couple of possible replacements. She had already identified two forged artifacts for him; how much more could they need from her? The realization brought her a mingled sense of relief and sadness. She had enjoyed working with the government on a secret project. Most of her work was meaningful to her but could never be considered interesting by most of the rest of the world. But working with spies had been exciting no matter who was doing the looking. Now that it was over, Jane felt as if she were returning to the real world. And then there was Blue.

For a moment, she'd thought maybe they had something, some spark, some connection. She was attracted to him, both physically and emotionally. He was funny, intelligent, and kind. And he had almost seemed to feel the same about her at some moments, especially when they were kissing. In reality, he was suspicious of her, distrustful. To feel that way about her, he must have kept himself emotionally unavailable and remote. Whatever she had sensed between them had either been one sided or a surface physical attraction. To be fair, she had practically thrown herself at him, had made the first move and kissed him. How many men wouldn't respond to that, if given the chance? She was disappointed and hurt, but she would move on. As long as she never, ever had to see him again. And why would she? Their worlds didn't intersect on a regular basis and likely never would again.

She showered, put on a pair of comfortable pants and hoodie and went into the living room. Nick was still there, sitting on the couch, staring at nothing.

"No Emily?" she asked.

"She's going out or something. Can't remember. Either way she won't be here," Nick replied.

"What are you doing?' Jane asked.

"Thinking about things," Nick said.

"What kind of things?" Jane asked. She curled her feet beneath her and sank onto the couch beside him.

"Big, important things," he replied.

"Like what big, important things?" Jane asked.

"Like how I hurt you, let you down, messed everything up."

"Oh, those are big things. But they're in the past. We've moved on," she assured him.

He swiped his hands over his face. "But that's the thing, Jane. I don't want to move on. I want to move forward."

"We've been over this," Jane said.

"There's one thing we haven't discussed," he said.

"What's that?" she asked, smiling.

In answer, he reached into his pocket, pulled out a little box, and opened it to reveal a diamond resting on a plush bed of satin. "Marry me."

Before Jane could summon a response, the door burst open and Blue was there. He looked flustered, distressed, panicked. His eyes scanned the room and landed on Jane.

"Get your things, you're coming with me."

CHAPTER 16

Blue arrived home a few hours after Jane but similarly exhausted. He turned on his computer and reached for a box of cereal, a bowl, and milk while it warmed up. After demolishing half a box of cereal, he would want nothing more than sleep, but he couldn't do that until he checked in with work and eased his mind about the encrypted message he'd seen on the dark web about Jane.

The dark web was a hacker's paradise, untraceable, easy to encrypt, the perfect place to buy and sell anything illegal. He found the site that mentioned Jane and plugged in his decryption key. It would take a while, given the innumerable possibilities. He ate a couple of bowls of cereal and pushed back in his chair, resting his feet on the desk. He would close his eyes while the decryption key did its thing.

Forty minutes later, the computer chimed, letting him know his program had hit on the correct combination to unlock the site. Blue sat up, yawning as he wiped the sleep from his eyes. He woke his monitor and leaned in to see what he'd uncovered and then his feet hit the floor with a bang.

He leaned in, practically pressing his nose to the monitor. Someone had ordered Jane's kidnapping, dead or alive but preferably alive. The fee was a hundred thousand dollars with a ten thousand dollar bonus if she was kept alive. Last night's kidnapping really had been about her and not him, but why? Was their case enough to put her life in so much danger? Whoever was doing the forgeries had to be making a killing, and somehow that money was being funneled into terror cells bent on wreaking havoc on the United States. Jane was one of the only people who could detect the forgeries and had, in fact, already detected two of them. She could put a serious dent in the operation, perhaps even bring it to a standstill. Of course she was a high value target. Now she was at her house, alone and unprotected. And Blue was the only person who knew how much danger she was in.

He dashed to his feet and grabbed his phone, but it was dead. He was supposed to charge it when he got home, but he fell asleep first. No matter, there was no time to call anyone besides Jane, and she certainly wouldn't take his call. Instead of worrying about his phone, he dashed to his room, unlocked his safe, and reached for his gun and holster.

The holster was something he'd bought on a whim, almost as a joke. At the time, he hadn't been able to imagine a situation he would need to use it. Now as he attempted to put it on over his t-shirt, he realized he had no idea how to wear it. Feeling like the world's worst secret agent, he returned to his computer and Googled, "How to fasten a holster." Once it was fastened, he added a hoodie over it to conceal it and then reached for his gun. He took two steps toward the door and remembered his gun wasn't loaded. Pivoting back to the safe, he grabbed the ammo, loaded the gun, and slid it back in the holster. Being a spy was exhausting. He had no idea how Ridge and Ethan made it look so easy. And he had never seen either of them hide a gun under a hoodie.

Once he was armed, he plugged his phone into the car charger and took off, double parked outside Jane's house, and sprinted up to her apartment. The one spy-tech gadget at his ready disposal was a computerized lock pick, something he could plug in and open any electronic lock. Jane had such a lock, he had absently noted on his first visit. He plugged his device in the keyhole, pushed a button, and the lock easily sprang open. Taking a breath to prep himself for whatever he might find inside, he pushed open the door.

Jane sat on the couch looking like she'd just stepped out of the shower, her temporary roommate, Nick, beside her. They both turned to survey Blue with shock. He said the first thing he could think of.

"Get your things, you're coming with me."

"No, I'm not. Go away," Jane said, frowning.

"I'm sorry, did that sound like a request? Get your things or don't, but either way you're coming with me."

She shook her head. He took a step inside and closed the door, securing it behind him. He grasped her hand, hauled her off the couch, marched her into her bedroom, and closed the door, leaning on it to prevent escape.

"Someone ordered a hit on you," he whispered. "You are in extreme danger. You need to leave now."

She paled slightly. "Someone wants me dead?"

"No, they want you alive, but that could be worse because I can't figure out why unless they plan to get information from you first. But the people who will respond to the ad will most likely end up killing you in the process of trying to take you in. We got lucky last night. We might not again. So gather enough stuff for a few days because we're leaving."

"Where are we going?"

Blue blinked at her. He hadn't thought that far ahead yet. "For now I'm going to get you out of here and then we'll see what Ridge wants to do with you."

"I don't like this," she said.

"Neither do I, but I'm not joking around. We need to be gone from here in two minutes, so pack your things."

Reluctantly she turned away from him, opened a few drawers and her closet, set some clothes on the bed, and began arranging them in a case. Blue saw the silk nightie she'd worn the night before in a sad little pile at the end of her bed and swallowed hard, remembering the feel and smell of her in it. She was mad, he could tell.

He'd try to deal with that later. For now he needed to focus on her safety.

He followed her into the bathroom while she gathered her toiletries, or what was left of them since most of her things were still at the hotel in New York. Blue had tried to get them for her, but the hotel assured them they would ship them home to her. She took a new toothbrush from beneath the sink, and then she was ready. "What am I going to say to Nick?" she whispered, more to herself than him.

"Tell him we're going away together," Blue suggested.

She shook her head. "Wouldn't work. He was privy to my emotional state when I arrived home." She sighed and rubbed the area between her eyes. "I'm going to have to tell him a little bit of what's going on."

"You can't."

"I can, and I will. If I'm in danger, then he's in danger. He needs to know to be careful, to keep an eye out for himself and for Emily."

"Are you purposely contradicting everything I say?" he asked.

"Not everything is about you," she said, bypassing him as she stalked toward the living room.

"I bet it's about me a little," he murmured to himself as he trotted to keep up.

"What's going on?" Nick asked, looking duly alarmed.

"There's been an incident. I'm in danger, and I need to go," Jane said. "You might be in danger also, so keep an eye on Emily for me, please."

Blue expected some sort of reaction. Instead Nick blinked at her, his face going the same shade of pale as hers. "Your dad?"

She shook her head. "Long story, I'll tell you when it's over." She stood on her toes and kissed his cheek.

"You didn't answer my question," he replied, picking her up and holding her at eye level.

"We'll talk more later," Jane said.

"Promise?"

"Promise."

"I'll hold you to it," Nick said. He squeezed her and let her go, giving Blue a look he couldn't discern. "Anything happens to her, I'll hold you personally responsible."

"Get in line," Blue said. He stepped in front of Jane, pulled his gun from its holster, hoping it looked smooth and not as clumsy as it felt. It would be his luck to drop the thing and accidentally shoot himself or one of them. Feigning confidence, he led the way through the door. Taking Jane's hand, he herded her down the stairs and to his car, keeping a wary eye out for anyone suspicious. The problem was that when he was really looking, everyone seemed suspicious. He began to feel some sympathy for Jane's decision to pepper spray him that first day. She was right—when you were vulnerable, everyone looked like a possible predator. And he had been following her that day, though not for any nefarious purpose. He must have looked scary to her, tall, tattooed, blue haired, and skulking behind her. Knowing how much danger she was in made everyone they passed look similarly sinister to him. He had to stay rational, to keep a cool head. It would be his luck to take down a nun or harmless falafel cart guy because he developed a panicky trigger finger.

They reached the car and he shut her inside before sprinting around to ease in behind the wheel. For a moment, he was tempted to slide across the top of the car, but he didn't want to risk his paint job or getting impaled on his hood ornament. Plus it was likely he would run out of momentum halfway through and end up crawling off the car like the dejected, non-athlete he was. A quick glance in the mirror showed no one in their wake. He would keep a close eye out as they drove to…where should he take her? Where was safe?

There was only one place he could think of. After a few circuitous false starts to make sure they weren't followed, he turned once again and headed home. His building had a garage, protected from the street. It was high security and, thanks to his job, completely off the radar.

"What is this place?" Jane asked as they parked underground and he retrieved her bag.

"This is my place," Blue said, pushing the button for the elevator.

Once they were inside and the doors were closed, he breathed a sigh of relief, took out his key, and put it in the elevator.

"You live in the penthouse?" she asked.

"Yes."

"Huh." She crossed her arms over her chest.

"What?" he prodded.

"I find it interesting a government employee drives a Jaguar, lives in a luxury penthouse, and you think *I'm* the one who is suspicious."

"I told you I sold an app," he said.

"So you say."

He scowled, not liking her inference. "Look, I could easily be making a solid six figures in the private sector. I could leave tomorrow and write my meal ticket in Silicon Valley. It's not like they haven't offered. Google practically begged me to... I stay because the work I do is important."

"What's the problem? Does it bother you when someone questions your intent, your very morality based on circumstantial evidence?" she said.

He opened his mouth to reply and closed it again when the elevator dinged. "Make yourself comfortable, I have to call work." He reached for his phone, thankful it had enough battery to make a call, while Jane meandered around his space. He tried to see it through her eyes. The space was grand, and it had a great view. Otherwise it looked like any twenty nine year old's bachelor pad—sparse, mismatched furniture and a couple of random pictures hung haphazardly on the walls. The only difference was that one entire wall was taken up with his massive computer and hard drives, powerful enough to allow him to work from home, if needed. The nature of his job didn't keep regular hours. Sometimes he needed to track what governments in different time zones were up to. Working from home allowed him to do that more comfortably.

"What now?" Ridge answered.

"Just making sure you didn't die laughing," Blue said.

"Jury's still out."

"There's a hit on Jane. I found it on the dark web, encrypted."

"I'll send a team for her," Ridge said.

"I already got her, she's here, at my house."

There was a pause. "You got her yourself?"

"It seemed critical and time sensitive, and my phone was dead."

Ridge clicked his tongue in disapproval. It was likely his phone had never died inconveniently. He probably always remembered to charge it and had a few backup phones just in case. As if to remind him how much of a super spy he wasn't, Blue's phone low-battery warning beeped ominously. Surreptitiously, he reached for his charger and plugged it in.

"She can't stay there. Ethan's coming home tomorrow. He'll take her to a safe house."

Blue eyed Jane, now paused in front of one of the pictures on his wall, inspecting it with the same intensity she did everything, including kiss. "I don't think so."

There was another pause. "You don't think so?"

"She would not be comfortable with Ethan," Blue said. And he would not be comfortable having her with Ethan. The last woman Ethan rescued fell in love with him. It was a job hazard for men like Ethan and Ridge. They couldn't help themselves. He saw the way women looked at them and responded to them, regardless of the fact that they were both now married, though secretly in Ethan's case. Women were programed to respond to masculine men, to heroes, to rescuers. Blue was none of those things.

"It's not about comfort; it's about safety," Ridge reminded him.

"She's safe here."

"But for how long? Eventually they're going to track her if she stays in the city. You know how it is; the intelligence community is tripping over itself here. Everything everywhere is wired, recorded, photographed. She needs to be out of the city."

"I'll take her," Blue heard himself volunteer, turning his back to Jane.

Ridge did the pause thing again. Sometimes it meant he was thinking, and sometimes it meant he was trying to keep a cap on his temper. Since Blue hadn't done anything to draw his ire for the moment, he figured he must be thinking.

"Let me ask you this, Blue, and I need an honest answer. If it came to it, could you kill a man to keep her safe?"

Blue turned to eye Jane again, now picking up a paperweight on his desk, turning it over and studying it as if it was one of her artifacts. "Yes."

"Okay, then. She's in your hands."

CHAPTER 17

Blue hung up with Ridge feeling slightly queasy. What had he just done? Jane's safety now rested solely in his hands, hands that were more accustomed to typing on a computer than punching someone or shooting a gun.

"So. It appears you may be stuck with me a while."

"Oh," Jane replied, setting down the paperweight.

"Try not to sound so thrilled," Blue said.

"I was thinking of quitting, actually. Before you showed up, I was going to call Mr. Ridge and tell him to find someone else."

"What? Why?" he exclaimed.

"Really, Blue, *really?*" she asked.

"Because we shared a few lighthearted kisses?" he said.

"Yes, that's exactly it. And then after those kisses you accused me of being a terrorist mastermind. It's hard to know, really, if it was the kisses or the suspicion of being an artifact-forging mass murderer. I'm going to have to think about it, come to a conclusion, and get back to you."

"In my defense, you've done nothing to help yourself prove you're not a terrorist," he said.

"You've done nothing to prove you're not Jimmy Hoffa. Maybe you are. Because how do you expect someone to prove a negative?"

"There's one easy way. Tell me why you have no digital footprint. Tell me why you're invisible."

"No," she stubbornly insisted.

"Why not? What possible reason could you have for not telling me, and what possible reason could you have for being invisible in the first place?"

"How dare I have a private life that's none of your concern?" she said. "I mean, we've known each other for almost two weeks now. You should definitely have the inside scoop on all my secrets."

"You expect me to trust you, but you won't give me anything to go on."

She picked up the paperweight again, seemed to consider chucking it at his head and, with effort, set it back down. "You have issues."

"I have issues? I'm not the one who stole a car and mysteriously flew home without a ticket or ID. I'm not the one who has no past, no history, no driver's license, no credit rating, no health or dental records, no social media. I don't have issues. You have issues." He pointed at her so she'd be clear on who he was talking about.

She put her hands on her hips, which would have been cute if he weren't so angry. She was pint-sized and adorable, way too much to ever be taken seriously as a credible threat. But she was trying her best with hands on hips and heaving, angry breathing. "None of those things are any of your business. No one normal looks into them upon meeting a new acquaintance."

He rolled his eyes. "Absolutely everyone looks into them. Maybe not as deep or as far or as I do, but everyone does it. Want to know someone's dating history? Check social media. Want to know someone's political affiliation? Check social media. Are you honestly trying to tell me you've never cyber stalked someone?"

"Never, not once. You know what I want to do when I want to get to know someone? I ask them questions about themselves and listen to their answers," she said.

"It's like you're speaking another language, one that died with the advent of the industrial age." Blue said. "Who does that, I mean, really? No one, that's who. Just because you work with antiquated artifacts doesn't mean you have to be antiquated in real life."

"You are being totally unfair, not just to me, but to all womankind. Do you think it's moral to show up for a date knowing a woman's credit rating and medical history? That's a despicable invasion of privacy."

"No, it's called being smart. And if I don't like what a woman's credit rating or medical history has to say, I don't show up for the date," he said.

Her jaw dropped. "That's horrible."

He tapped his temple. "That's smart; that's safe. You can't go by what someone says. People lie all the time. The only truth is what's online where people are real and reveal themselves."

"Really? Like how people are real on Instagram and Facebook? You know what Nick's profile says? That he has a PhD, an interest in vintage cars, and holds material possessions loosely. You know what the reality is? That he's been in school for ten years, works as a valet on the weekends, and sleeps on my couch. Don't tell me people are real online. That's what avatars are for, to keep people from being real."

"Leave avatars out of it. They've done nothing to you," he said.

"Are you trying to joke with me when we're in the middle of an argument?"

"I can't help it. You're so stinking cute. It's like trying to stay mad at a chipmunk," he said.

"Strange, I'm having no trouble maintaining my anger at you," she said.

"Come on, Jane, we might as well be friends. We're stuck with each other for the foreseeable future," he cajoled. She didn't respond, but neither did she throw the paperweight she kept eyeing. Blue took a step closer. "Tell me why I can't find you online."

Jane took a step closer. "If I drank poison, and the only way to get the antidote was to tell you the reason I'm not online, I would gladly perish. I would rather have my wisdom teeth put back in and taken out again with no anesthetic than ever clear up this mystery for you."

"I'm going to take that as a maybe," Blue said.

"Here's what I'll give you: You can ask me anything else, anything that doesn't pertain to my lack of online presence, and I'll tell you. I'm an open book for people who seek answers."

"What does your father do?" he asked.

She shook her head.

"Do you still think I'm cute?" he tried.

"It's waning," she said.

"That's weird because I think you're definitely getting cuter," he said.

"Now that you're certain I'm not a terrorist, you mean?"

"Who says I'm certain? Maybe I like to live dangerously." He rested his right hand on her shoulder, his thumb caressing her neck.

"I can't do this with you."

"Because I called you a terrorist? That was hours ago. Are you ever going to let it go and move on?" His left hand settled on her hip.

"When you unceremoniously broke into my apartment—by the way, guy who's into modern technology, we have these things called doorbells now—I was in the middle of being proposed to."

"By the hobo who sleeps on your couch? Do homeless men often ask you to marry them? Is that some type of payment plan you've worked out? He gets to live in your apartment on the condition that he makes an honest woman of you?"

"Nick and I dated off and on for ten years," she said.

"Ten years and he's only now trying to seal the deal? He *is* a catch. You'd better run back there right now and put the ring on before another decade goes by."

"I don't remember asking for your input on my love life."

"Baby, for the last couple of weeks, I *am* your love life," he reminded her, leaning in for a kiss she returned with interest, standing on her toes and gripping his shirt to tug him closer.

The kiss ended and he rested his forehead on hers. "Jane," he whispered.

"Mm," she said.

"How did you get back to DC?"

With a growl of frustration, she shoved him away. "No."

"You don't understand. I've spent my entire life on a computer, trying to solve riddles and puzzles, and I have never failed. And then you come along and you're like some kind of walking Rubik's cube."

"I guess you have a decision to make. Do you want to get to know the real woman standing before you, or do you want to solve the mystery of my lack of virtual history?"

"I'm a hacker. *Hacker Monthly* named me one of the top ten hackers in the world."

"Really?" she asked.

"No, but they probably would, if such a thing or magazine existed. The point is this is what I do, and I'm amazing at it. Asking me not to care about it is like asking a surgeon not to cut out a tumor."

"Am I the tumor in this scenario?" she asked.

"You're the everything in this scenario. Lately it's like my life has reoriented itself and centered on you. I've gone from deep loathing to deep liking so quickly I have emotional whiplash. But I can't take not knowing who or what you are."

"Well, there you go," Jane said.

"Just tell me," he pled.

"No."

"Well, there you go," he said. They stared at each other, a sad, impenetrable distance between them. "Don't marry the guy who took ten years to realize what a good thing he had going all along."

Jane didn't say what she was thinking, that he was asking her to hope instead for the guy who preferred a virtual woman to the real one standing in front of him.

<h1 style="text-align:center">CHAPTER 18</h1>

The next morning they set off. The ride was silent and awkward, as the previous night had been. Last night they ordered takeout Chinese, and the reminder of their perfect date in New York was painful.

Now Jane sat staring out the window watching the scenery in silence. No one could do quiet like Jane, Blue thought. Her entire body became still so it was difficult to discern if she was even breathing. Blue wondered why she did that. Finally it occurred to him to ask.

"Why do you sit so still?"

"When we lived in Africa, a boy I knew was learning to hunt. His dad taught us how to stalk, how to track, how to be silent. I loved it, thought it was the greatest thing ever, and I practiced so much I guess I internalized everything."

"Did you ever see a lion?"

"Yes. When I lived there, it was the last age of the Massai lion hunts. They don't do it anymore. They have an Olympics style contest instead. I'm not going to say I condone or endorse lion hunting, because I don't, but it was something to see. I liked the pageantry of it, the ceremony and tradition."

"How many places have you lived?"

"I don't know. We moved a lot when I was a kid, but what makes it interesting was the manner of places I lived. They were always fascinating in vastly different ways. I don't know how I turned out so ordinary."

His mind flashed to her bashing in a car's window and shoving a screwdriver in the starter. "I don't think you did."

"Compared to my sisters, I did. They're…extremely unusual."

"How so?" he asked.

"My older sister was a wild child, seriously insane. She had no fear. She still doesn't."

"What does she do?"

"She followed in our father's footsteps," Jane said, turning to gaze out the window. Was she sad or merely pondering?

"Doing…" he prompted, but Jane shook her head. "You said you had two sisters."

"My younger sister is sweeter, but no tamer," she said and left it at that. "Are you going to tell me where we're going?"

"Somewhere safe," he said.

"And that is…" she prompted.

He was tempted to shake his head, to keep her as in the dark as he was. But she'd learn soon enough where they were headed.

"My parents' house."

Jane sat up. "Are you sure that's safe? I don't want to put them in danger."

"It's safe," Blue assured her, but she still looked concerned. "Hey, it's safe." He patted her knee, and she did the flinching thing again. His lips pressed together, concealing his smile.

"Don't be smug," Jane snapped.

"Smug, me? Why would I be smug? Because you jump at the mere brush of my hand on your body? Because you have no way of hiding your undying attraction to me? Why would that end in any sort of smugness?"

"You've got it all wrong. I *used* to be attracted to you. Now I'm annoyed."

"You jumped because you were annoyed by my touch?" he asked.

"Yes, and the more you push it, the more it's veering into repulsion," she said.

"You're a bad liar," he said.

"I'm an amazing liar," she said, so deadpan he glanced at her with narrowed, speculative eyes. "Look at you, looking at me. You're still not convinced I'm not a terrorist, are you?"

"I'm mostly sure," he said uncertainly. "There's only like a one percent doubt. Maybe two."

"Unbelievable," she said, facing forward with a huff of frustration.

"Hey, at least I'm being honest with you. I'm not saying there's no doubt in my mind. And I find you crazy hot even though you might be a killer. Doesn't that count for something?"

"I am so sick of men who believe they're doing me a favor by being interested in me. You know I have a doctorate and a dream job at one of the world's preeminent museums? And yet I have you believing you're throwing me a bone by being physically attracted to me and Nick thinking he's king of the castle because he keeps coming back to me between episodes of cheating."

"That guy cheated on you? Seriously, Jane, you can't marry him. And for the record, I would never cheat on you. That's completely wrong."

"You think I cheated on the entire United States Government," she exclaimed.

"Only a little. And I'm more than physically attracted to you. Is that all you think this is?"

"I don't think this is anything. As for cheating, what do you think it is when you go behind my back and try to snoop on me?" she asked.

"Do you honestly believe infidelity and looking up information about a person are the same?" he asked.

"No, but I believe they're similar. They're both a matter of breaking trust."

"No," Blue said, shaking his head.

"Yes. If I had an online presence, you should have no right to it. It would be personal, private, and off-limits to you."

"My job," he began, but she interrupted him.

"I'm not talking about your job. Your job is to hunt terrorists, and I get that. There are bad guys and no-goodniks in the world. Have at 'em, go get them. Peer into every aspect of their lives and destroy them forever. But private citizens are just that, private. You should not be looking; it's a gross invasion."

He shook his head but otherwise didn't reply. The remainder of the ride was silent. A while later they pulled up in front of a house in his suburban Philly neighborhood.

"Jane," he said softly. He rested his hand on her thigh and she predictably jumped. "I know you're mad at me right now, but can you do one little thing for me?"

"What's that?" she asked, her tone wary.

"Tell me what a no-goodnik is," he said, and she smiled.

"Don't be one, and you'll never have to find out." She faced the house, her smile dimming slightly. "I'm a little nervous to meet your family."

"They're nice, I promise," he said.

"It's not them; it's me. I'm not so great at meeting new people."

"Did you bring your pepper spray?" he asked.

"Of course not," she said.

"Then I'm sure it will be fine," he said.

"No, it probably won't. I hear normal words in my head, but then social anxiety steps in and says, 'Not today, human. Let's be weird instead,' and what ends up coming out is a bunch of mixed up words and phrases that make no rational sense. Or, worse, I come off as mean or uptight, and I'm neither of those things."

He took her hand in both his and began smoothing his palm over it in a relaxing manner. "What would help, Jane?"

"Not having the expectation to speak until I'm ready, until I've warmed up. Being put on the spot triggers an uncontrollable anxiety response."

"What if I could guarantee it won't be a problem for you not to talk until you're ready?"

"That's not possible," Jane said.

"Oh, but it is," Blue countered.

"How?" she asked.

"You'll see." He let her hand go and opened his door. Reluctantly, she opened her door and tagged behind.

CHAPTER 19

An hour in, Jane hadn't said a word. And nobody noticed. Blue's mother, however, hadn't stopped talking since they arrived.

"Oh, my goodness, Jane, so nice to meet you. Are you really a doctor? What am I saying, of course you are. Women can be those now; women can be anything. Although I'm not sure what the difference is between an archeologist and an anthropologist. What is the difference? I'd really like to know. Anyway, you can use this room right down the hall. It hasn't been used in years because everyone we know lives local so we don't get a lot of company who stay over night. Blue will stay in his old room, of course. We left it as it was, not as some sort of monument, but more out of laziness. My husband works odd hours, I'm sure Blue's told you, and the last thing he wants to do when he gets home is a house project. Not that I'm complaining because I'm not, and I'm sort of not into house stuff myself, unless I get some random idea while watching HGTV. For a while, I wanted to shiplap everything, and then I realized how much work that was and gave up. Do you have shiplap in your house? Although you probably don't have a house, living in DC. Philly is more suburban, I think. It seems like everything in DC is citified, and I can't get used to those tall townhomes. I'm glad Blue doesn't live in one of those. So many stairs, and why would anyone want a kitchen on a separate level than your seating area? Although I do worry what would happen if the electric ever went out, being on the top floor and all. He's probably got a plan for that, I try not to interfere…"

She continued talking, almost without breathing. Behind her back, Blue made eye contact and smiled as if to say, "See, I told you."

When there was a pause in the one-sided conversation, Jane opened her mouth to say thank you or even hello, but his mother resumed talking.

"Have you met Tad yet? What am I saying, of course you haven't. He'll be here later for supper. Are you hungry? Have you eaten? Well, it doesn't matter, I'm serving supper nonetheless. I made Blue's favorites because I so rarely get him home for supper, not that I'm complaining. Who am I kidding, of course I am. Come home once in a while, kiddo," she paused to tap Blue's cheek before continuing. "Anyway, I think you're really going to like Tad. He's such a sweet, gentle…" she walked out of the room, still talking. Blue closed the door behind her and leaned on it.

"Isn't she going to notice we're no longer there?" Jane asked.

"Once when I was seven, she left me at a gas station and it took her two hours to notice. And another time my brother and I had a wager going about how long we could go without saying a word before she noticed. We both gave up after three days of not talking."

"Wow," Jane said.

"In her defense, she's on a break from work. On school days, she's gets all the chattiness out in the classroom. And she teaches first grade, so it's sort of imperative she talk all day."

"You don't need to defend her to me. I think she seems lovely," Jane said. The talking was a bit incessant, but otherwise she seemed like a warm, genuine person. Her eyes traveled around the room, his room. "So, the inner sanctum."

"It's about time I had a girl in here, although I think some people I went to high school with probably would have had bets on it being after I turned thirty," he said.

"I can't be the first girl who has ever been in your room," Jane said.

He nodded. "Sadly, yes."

"That reminds me. You still owe me a viewing of your middle school picture," she said.

He closed his eyes and groaned. "Please no."

"Don't be a welcher, Bishop. Let me see the goods."

"I'm already regretting this," he said, reaching for a shelf that contained his old yearbooks. He flipped a few pages and turned the book to face her.

"Oh, no," Jane said. She reached for the book and drew it closer, squinting. "I had no idea people actually wore headgear."

"What?" he asked, coming alongside her for a better view. "That's not me. That kid is Asian. That's me." He pointed a few spaces away.

"Oh," she drawled. "Aw, you were so cute."

"You can say it—I was fat."

"You were fluffy," she amended. "Besides, you seem to have…" she trailed off, her eyes traveling the expanse of him.

"Oh, geez," Blue said. He took the book, tossed it away, and kissed her. Eventually a sound from the kitchen startled them apart.

"How do you do that?" he asked.

"What, kiss? You press your lips softly together. I'm surprised you're asking because you kind of seem to know what you're doing. In fact, you're rather amazing at it," she said.

"No, I mean I don't even know who you are, really. I only half trust you, I'm more than halfway mad at you, still not sure you didn't have me kidnapped, know for certain you left me at the airport with my hands tied, but I get within five feet of you and lose all control."

"You think you've got problems? The guy I like thinks I'm a criminal," she said.

"Are you?" he asked, only half joking.

In answer, she stood on her toes and kissed him. He responded, his hands reaching for her, pulling her closer.

"Blue, Mom wanted me to…oh, hello." The door to the bedroom opened and a man poked his head inside. He looked similar to Blue, but his hair was sandy blond and he was shorter and more muscular.

They were kind of like a before and after of someone who was put on a rack and stretched. "I'm Tad."

Startled and flustered, Jane said the first thing that popped to mind. "I'm not a criminal."

"No, I know," Tad agreed. "Pennsylvania decriminalized kissing last year, so you've caught a lucky break. Still doesn't explain who you are or why you're kissing my brother."

"This is Jane, a…colleague," Blue said.

"Okay. I'm going to pretend that long pause in front of the word colleague was in no way suspicious. Hi, Jane, I'm Tad." He stepped forward and offered up his hand to shake.

"Hi, I'm Jane," Jane replied.

"Jane was it?" Tad said, touching his finger to his ear as if to hear her better.

"It's short for 'Incredibly Awkward When Meeting New People.' I'd like to say it gets better, but it takes about a decade," Jane said. "In ten years, I'm going to come across as really smooth and polished."

"Something to look forward to," Tad said. "In the meantime, Mom wanted me to tell you supper is ready."

"Thanks, we'll be there in a minute," Blue said.

Tad nodded and eased out of the room.

"He seemed remarkably incurious about the fact that he walked in on you kissing someone. Has that happened a lot?"

"Literally all the time," Blue said. "I mean, you've seen my middle school pictures. The ladies were lining up to get a piece of me. I have three on standby in the closet for after you leave." He took her hand and drew it to his chest. "Does that make you jealous, Jane?"

"Do you want me to be jealous, Blue?"

"Kind of. Not like snatch someone's hair off her head crazy person level jealous, but maybe secretly Facebook stalk my exes level jealous."

"I don't have a Facebook account," she reminded him.

"And why is that again? I can't remember," he said, kissing her palm as he feigned ignorance.

"Aren't we going to be late for supper?" she asked, easing her arms around his waist.

"Yes, but something tells me it's going to be worth it." She tipped her face to his as he bent to kiss her.

"Blue!" his mother yelled.

Blue broke away. "That's the 'I'm running out of patience' yell. We have to respond to that one." He opened the door for her and allowed her to precede him through. Everyone was already seated at the loaded table when they arrived.

"Sorry," Blue murmured, as they took their seats at the table.

"I don't think I've been introduced," Blue's father said. He was a combination of his two sons—as tall as Blue but as solidly built as Tad, a hulking barrel of a man—but his voice was quiet and soft, his manner gentle. Jane wondered if he was as quiet and soft spoken as his wife was not.

"This is Jane, my, er, coworker," Blue stumbled again. "Jane, my dad, Will Bishop."

"Hi, Mr. Bishop, thank you for having me, it's nice to meet you," Jane said, trying hard not to mumble or stutter or say anything outlandishly odd. She could usually get through the preliminary greetings okay. It was everything after that scrambled somewhere between her brain and lips. In her mind, she was a witty and gifted conversationalist. In reality, she was often…not.

Under the table, Blue's hand rested on her leg, soothing her with soft, gentle passes.

"It's a pleasure to meet you, Jane. You're very welcome to be here," Will said. "And thank you for complying with our odd eating schedule."

Jane had no idea what he was talking about until she glanced at the clock and saw it was only three in the afternoon.

"Dad and Tad are firefighters," Blue explained. "They're always coming and going on odd and different schedules. We eat when we can."

"I hadn't actually noticed the time," Jane admitted.

"You must have been wonderfully preoccupied," Tad said, and Jane felt her cheeks flush pink. Blue squeezed her leg and let it go as the food began to pass.

When his mother was certain everyone had received each dish of food, she began to talk again, the incessant chatter of someone who has no idea they're monopolizing the conversation. The men at the table seemed so used to it they hardly paid attention. Jane was thankful for it because it meant the pressure was off her to speak. She was safe to sit back, relax, and make her observations about the family.

She found it interesting Blue chose a profession so very far from that of his father and brother. Not much was as opposite from fire-fighting as hacking. On the other hand, they were all public servants. Blue had sacrificed what could potentially be a high six-figure annual salary to work for the government. And they seemed to think no less of him for it. There was no teasing, no one-upmanship. Of course there also wasn't much chance to get any of that in with their mother's unending stream of one-sided conversation.

"Blue, how's Maggie?" she asked about a half hour in and actually seemed to want an answer. She paused, regarding him with a thoughtful stare.

"She's fine, Mom," Blue said, shifting uncomfortably. "Still happily married."

Jane studied Blue's profile, wondering over his sudden discomfort. He steadily avoided her gaze, focusing instead on his nearly empty plate.

His mother clucked her tongue with what sounded like disapproval. "I still say you should have told her how you felt before she got married."

"Mom, I really don't want to talk about it," Blue said.

"All I'm saying is that when you're in love with someone you tell them. At the very least, you'll have a definitive answer," his mother said.

"I think the fact that she married another man was a definitive answer," Tad said.

"But that's only because she didn't know Blue's in love with her. Personally I think they would have been a good match. They have more in common than she and Ridge do. I've given this a lot of thought."

"Mom, I'd really like to move on from this conversation," Blue said.

"Why?" His mother asked. "You never want to talk about personal things. We have no idea what's going on with you unless we check social media. What's so wrong with talking about your problems with your family?"

Blue gave Jane a significant look, one his mother couldn't help but notice.

"What? You said you two are friends. Does your friend not know you're in love with Maggie?" his mother questioned.

"Oh, boy, Mom, you're really digging a pit here," Tad chimed in.

"Change the conversation, Dorothy," Will piped up, giving his wife a look.

"Why does everyone keep saying…?" Her eyes fell on Blue and Jane again, speculatively this time. "Oh. Dear me. So." Her lips sealed then. It was as if when she needed mindless chatter the most, the power failed her.

To try and cover the awkwardness, Will and Tad launched into a conversation about some issue at their respective fire stations, but it was clear they were unaccustomed to being the ones who talked. Eventually all talk came to an end, but, mercifully, so did the meal.

"Maybe you'd like to show Jane the patio," his mother suggested.

Wordlessly, Blue stood, led the way to the porch, and held the door for Jane.

CHAPTER 20

They sat on the patio and gazed silently at the back yard.

"That went well," Blue said after a long time of silence. "I think the only way it could have gone better is if my mom pantsed me and then gave me an atomic wedgie while everyone watched."

Jane gave a little half laugh, somewhere between amusement and exasperation.

"The thing with Maggie, it's not as if it ever had a chance to get off the ground. She was Ridge's from the get go. I know that; I've always known that. It's always been one more nail in my coffin of doomed romances."

"Like me," Jane said.

"No, Jane, not like you. That's what makes it interesting. Nothing has ever clicked before the way it does with you," he said.

"But does it though, really? What about us has worked? Me physically assaulting you? You being only eighty percent certain I'm not a terrorist?"

"It's up to about ninety," he said.

"We're attracted to each other. The physical chemistry works, but at some point you have to ask yourself if that's enough. You have your overt dependence on virtual reality, I have social anxiety."

"The social anxiety doesn't faze me," he assured her.

"I also have Nick."

He scowled. "That fazes me."

"It's not allowed to faze you; I'm not yours. You're in love with another woman. You don't trust me. Those two things have been made abundantly clear to me. So, really, what are we doing here? What's the point of all this?"

"It's more than physical attraction. I like you. You're funny and smart and cool. I think it's cute how you have a PhD and yet get flustered when talking to ordinary strangers. And the Maggie thing is one of those things I have to work through. It's not like it has any future, but the heart wants what it wants sometimes, and lately it's been saying it wants you."

"Even though you don't know who I am and I'm not online?" she reminded him.

He opened his mouth to say something, thought better of it, and closed his mouth again. The truth was it did bother him that she wasn't online; it bothered him a lot. But everything else he said to her was true, too, and when he was with her, he forgot. He forgot everything—his job, her potential criminal ties, his feelings for Maggie, her lack of virtual footprint. All he knew was when he was with her his heart felt full and whole and he wanted that feeling to continue.

"I don't want to lose what we have going here," he said eventually.

"What do we have going here? You can't even bring yourself to say I'm anything but your coworker. So let that be it. We're coworkers. Maybe at the end of this we'll be friends, but let's not fool ourselves we're anything else because eventually one of us is going to get hurt, and it seems like we've both been hurt too many times to let it happen again."

Blue wasn't ready to agree, wasn't ready to let go. The one thing they had going for them was time. Maybe with enough time on their side, they could get things right. Instead of trying to talk her into giving them a chance, he would find another way to convince her; he would charm her into submission. He had never been able to do that before, but there was a definite first time for everything. All he knew was that, while not ready to give in completely and let go of his reser-vations, he was also not ready to give up on them entirely. They had something; he was sure of it, and he was certain Jane felt it, too.

"Let's recap," she suggested.

"Yes," he agreed.

"You're in love with another woman," she said.

"Yes."

"And I have a pending proposal from my ex-boyfriend of ten years."

"Yes."

"You can't trust me completely, both because you're not certain I'm not a criminal, but mostly because I lack a virtual footprint."

"Yes."

"I'm angry with you because you won't let go of your distrust."

"Yes?" he said, but that time it came out sounding like a question. He couldn't say for certain what she felt, only that it was something that kept her from giving in to him, to them.

"We agree there are too many issues between us," she said.

"Yes."

They were quiet a few seconds, their eyes on the horizon as a not-so-subtle tension began to wind between them, coiling like a snake.

"You're going to kiss me now, aren't you?" she asked.

"Yes."

He reached for her, but she held up a hand and leaned away. "I think I should call Charles."

"To tell him I'm going to kiss you? I'd prefer to keep it between us," Blue said.

"To tell him I'm in danger, to tell him he might be in danger. Plus I'd like to meet with him, to pick his brain and see if he has any idea what's going on."

Blue sat back. "No."

"I don't understand that word as you think it relates to me," she said.

"This is a sensitive operation. You can't tell anyone about it," he said.

"I don't have to tell him everything, but I can give him a heads up, see if he has any ideas about what might be going on. Why are you shaking your head at me?"

"I don't think it's a good idea for you to meet with him," Blue said.

"Why not?"

"Because he has a thing for you. You guys clearly have chemistry."

Jane put her hand to her head. "Are you actually telling me you don't want me to meet with my friend of twenty years because you're jealous?"

"No, of course not."

"Then why?" she asked.

"Because I don't want you to meet with your friend of twenty years because I'm jealous," he said. "I don't know where that immature possessiveness came from, sorry. It's just that you and he seemed to have chemistry, a connection, and my kneejerk reaction is to hide you away from him."

"I'm not interested in Charles," she said. "But even if I were, it wouldn't matter. You and I are not together. You have zero claim on my time or attention."

"I know. You're right, you're totally and completely right. Just like you're not jealous that I have a thing for Maggie."

"Right, except I kind of completely am," Jane said, frowning. "What is wrong with us?"

"I don't know, but I'm inclined to blame you," Blue said. "I was doing fine until you came along, pepper sprayed me, and made me like you."

"You were doing fine mooning over your married coworker?" she said.

"We had a system. I love her, and she, oblivious to my feelings, treats me like a brother."

"Sounds healthy," Jane said.

"Tell me again how your ex-boyfriend of a decade sleeps on your couch," he replied.

"So maybe neither of us has a positive frame of reference for relationships," she agreed. "That's why it's best we've decided to be friends."

"You decided. I never agreed to that," he said.

"We're talking in circles. Can I use your phone to call Charles?" He had confiscated her phone in case there was a trace on it.

He considered not giving the phone to her, but there was nothing to be gained by it. "You have his number memorized?" he said instead.

"I'll call his work number and leave a message," she replied.

With a sigh, he gave her his phone and watched while she found the number for the museum and left a message for Charles Stevens. "He might not even call," Jane said when she was finished. "I have no idea how regularly he checks his work messages." She had just finished speaking when the phone rang and Charles's number came up on the screen. Jane put him on speakerphone.

"Janie, what's up?"

"I'm in town."

"You are?"

"I'd like to see you."

"You would?" he said.

"You're mocking me," she said.

"I am?" he replied, chuckling. "Of course I want to see one of my favorite people. I'm free tonight. Want to meet for supper?"

Jane looked at Blue. They had already eaten supper, but it was only five. She would likely be hungry again in a few hours. Blue nodded. "Sure. My...colleague will be joining us."

"Um, weird but okay," he said. "What is this about?"

"I'd rather talk it out in person," Jane replied.

"So mysterious, Jane."

"You know me, Charles. A thrill a minute," Jane said.

"A family trait," he replied.

They made arrangements at a restaurant of Blue's choosing and disconnected. Blue checked his watch. "We have a while until we meet."

"Three hours isn't so much," Jane replied.

"It's enough to show you some of the finer parts of Philly," Blue said.

"Are you suggesting we go out? Like a, what's the word, date?" Jane said.

"I sort of owe you one, and the pressure's on to make it good," Blue said.

"All right," Jane agreed.

He leaned forward to kiss her, and the folding chair beneath him collapsed, tossing him haphazardly onto the deck. "You don't believe in omens, do you?" he asked, staring up at her from his new position on the ground.

"No," Jane replied, but later they would both begin to rethink their disbelief.

CHAPTER 21

Blue had three hours to show Jane the iconic Philadelphia and to make it as interesting as she had made New York for him. His brain went into panic mode, unable to think of anything, so he texted Tad and asked for advice.

If you could only show an outsider one Philly thing what would it be?

Tad's answer had determined their current destination.

Jane gasped when she realized where they were, and he knew he'd made the right choice. They climbed up the steps, all seventy two of them. Blue stopped at the top and turned to face the city, but Jane kept going, reaching for the door.

"Oh, no, it's closed," she said, her face peering in the window.

"What are you talking about?" he asked.

"The Art Museum. It's closed," she said.

"That's why you think we're here?" he asked.

"It's not?" she countered.

"No. *Rocky.* The steps." He pointed to the stairs, all leg-numbing seventy two of them.

She cocked her head at him. "Huh?"

"These stairs are the most famous landmark in Philly," he said.

"More famous than the Liberty Bell? Independence Hall? Betsy Ross? Literally anything connected to Ben Franklin?" she said.

"Oh," he drawled. "Right, you're smart. I forgot. But, still, *Rocky*? I mean, come on, Jane, *Rocky*."

She raised her hand and pointed to the top of her head. "Girl who grew up in Africa and has no idea what you're talking about."

"You seriously don't know what *Rocky* is?" he asked, aghast.

"No, but I've ridden an elephant and watched a baby giraffe be born," she offered helpfully.

"Your life is completely lacking," he said. "Okay, next thing then." He pressed his fingers to his temple, trying to think of something smart to impress her. He snapped his fingers. "I've got it. Come on." He took her hand and dragged her back down the seventy two steps.

"Wait," Jane called, leaning against the wall to massage her calves. "Charley horse. One hundred forty four steps are a lot."

"Lots of people run them," he told her.

"Why?" she asked.

"We really have to have a movie night at some point. Do you even know who Sylvester Stallone is?" Blue asked.

"*Rambo.*"

He blinked at her. "How do you know *Rambo* but not *Rocky*?"

"*Rambo* is my dad's favorite movie," she said.

"I didn't know *Rambo* was anyone's favorite movie," Blue said. He was hoping she would say more about her dad, whom he had deduced was likely a criminal, given her strange reaction every time he was mentioned, but she shrugged, smiling. "Come on, Secret Squirrel," he said, leading the way back to the car.

Traffic was its usual nightmare. They would barely have enough time to see the thing he was trying to show her. They were almost there, but as they drew nearer, the street was closed off with multiple police cars blocking the entrance. Blue turned on the radio and heard there had been a drive by shooting. He sighed.

"That's Poe's house," he pointed. "You can almost make out a glimpse of it, if you squint."

Jane pressed her face to the window, squinting. "That's cool."

"No, it's not. It's sad and pathetic. I was trying to show you the fun parts of Philly, but all you saw were a bunch of stairs and a possible murder. And now we're going to be late for your meeting."

"Don't worry about it," she said, resting her hand on his arm. "Besides, we'll always have cheesesteak."

"I don't remember the cheesesteak; I remember our first kiss," he said.

"The word 'first' implies more will continue," she said.

"I want them to, you know that, Jane," he said.

She shook her head. "You don't know what you want."

"I know what I don't want, and that is for you to marry a guy you don't love," he said.

Jane stared out her window, doing the completely still and silent thing.

"Do you see any lions out there?" Blue asked.

"Just the Nittany variety," she said, and he laughed.

"Right state, wrong city," he clarified.

They arrived at the restaurant Blue chose for them to meet Charles. It had been a trendy hangout years ago when he lived in Philly. Now it looked as though it had seen better days, but he wasn't willing to admit one more failure in his agenda so they left the car, entered the restaurant, and saw Charles already waiting for them at a table.

He stood to greet Jane with an enveloping hug and kiss on the cheek before extending his hand for Blue to shake. They sat, and a waitress came to take their drink order.

"What's good here?" Charles asked.

"Back in the day it used to be their burgers, but now..." Blue trailed off looking at the dirty establishment.

"A burger seems safe," Charles said, closing his menu.

"Not if you're a cow," Jane commented, and Charles grinned at her as if it were the cutest joke he'd ever heard. Or maybe the cutest joke teller. Blue scowled at his menu, also deciding on a burger.

"What are you having?" Jane asked.

"Also a burger," Blue replied.

She touched her hand to his leg, and he jumped. "I'm going to slip to the restroom. Can you order for me? I'll have whatever you're having."

"Sure," he said, but his eyes trailed after her, troubled. She had used the bathroom before they left home, not more than an hour ago. Did she have a tiny bladder, or was it something else? Worse than Jane's disappearance was the fact that he was now left alone with Charles Stevens.

"So," Charles said.

Blue stared at him, waiting for more.

"Awkward," Charles replied. "The ex-boyfriend, the future prospect."

"Jane said you had one date," Blue replied.

"Jane remembers things differently. Did she not tell you I was her first ever kiss?"

Blue squinted. "I thought you guys went out a year ago, but Jane had a boyfriend for ten years."

"I was before the boyfriend. This was back in the day, in Africa. She was fifteen, I was eighteen. I had known her since she was a little girl, and one day I realized she was all grown up. I also realized how much we had in common, and so we kissed. It was epic."

"No, she didn't tell me," Blue said, not admitting how much he didn't know about Jane. "Her life is extremely unusual."

"You have no idea," Charles replied.

"What's up with the dad?" Blue asked.

Charles narrowed his eyes in speculation. "You don't know?" Blue shook his head. "You haven't met him?" Blue shook his head again. "You should keep it that way. Because he'll kill you." It sounded like the kind of thing people said flippantly, when they were trying to be funny. But Charles wasn't smiling, and he didn't look amused. He sipped his water, and the two men sat in silence until the waitress arrived. After she left, Jane returned.

"Everything all right, Janie?" Charles asked.

"Yes," Jane assured them both.

"Good. Then tell me what's up," Charles demanded. "Why are you in Philly?"

Jane took a breath. "Where to begin? I seem to have stumbled into a bit of danger."

Charles blinked at her. "Your dad?"

She shook her head. "My own design this time. I've been verifying artifacts, and it's ruffled a few feathers. Blue and I came here until things cooled down."

Charles looked between Jane and Blue. "I think you should stay with me."

She shook her head. "I'm fine." Their food arrived, and they started to eat in silence a few minutes until Charles spoke again.

"Jane, you don't know you're safe, and I would feel better if you stayed with me."

"She's staying with me," Blue inserted.

"Her lab assistant?" Charles said, his tone derisive.

"I'm not her lab assistant," Blue said.

"What are you?" Charles asked, leaning forward a bit.

"Systems analyst and software engineer," Blue replied.

"Oh, well clearly you're prepared to keep her safe from a cyber attack. In the meantime, she should be with me," Charles replied.

"I'm sorry, Doctor Stevens, but how is an anthropologist supposed to keep her safe? Are you planning to dig up an attacker and dust him with tiny brushes?" Blue asked. He may not be a super spy, but at least he was trained and armed.

Instead of answering directly, Charles looked at Jane. "Tell him, Jane."

Jane sighed. "Charles was a mercenary."

Blue looked between them, dumbfounded. He had researched Charles Stevens, of course, and found him to be squeaky clean. He appeared to be like any other PhD anthropologist, if a bit more boring than most. And now they were telling him he had a hidden, secret past? "What? When was this?"

"In Africa, from eighteen to twenty one," Charles said.

"You kissed a teenage Jane when you were a mercenary?" Blue exclaimed.

"You told him about that?" Jane directed to Charles.

"He asked about you. What was I supposed to do, lie?" Charles said.

Now she turned to Blue. "You asked *him* about me? You're supposed to ask me about me."

"Fine, Jane. Why did you date a mercenary? Why do you *know* a mercenary?" Blue said.

"I know a lot of people," she snapped before returning her attention to Charles. "You are not allowed to tell him things about me. *Anything* about me." She gave him a significant look.

Charles was smiling as his gaze bounced between them. "You two aren't together," he surmised.

"We're…colleagues," Jane hedged.

"We're more than that," Blue said, massaging the throbbing pain between his eyes.

"Not much," Jane said, sighing. "The point is, Charles, have you heard anything on your end about forgeries? About danger?"

Charles laughed. "Janie, you must be joking. The most excitement in my day is balancing my budget. I'm more of an administrator now than I would care to admit. But I'm serious, I want you to stay with me until this all blows over." He reached for her hand, holding it between both of his.

"She's not staying with you, she's staying with me," Blue replied, resting a possessive hand on Jane's leg.

"Maybe let's let Jane decide," Charles said.

Jane looked between the two men. She opened her mouth to say something, and the window behind them exploded in a spray of glass.

CHAPTER 22

All three of them dove to the ground beneath the table as pandemonium broke out in the restaurant.

"I think that was a bullet," Blue said.

"I think so, too," Charles agreed.

"It could have been another drive by," Jane added. They weren't exactly in the chicest part of Philly.

"That's not a chance I'm willing to take," Blue replied.

"Me neither," Charles agreed. They settled Jane between them and herded out of the restaurant's back entrance on their hands and knees. Once they were outside, Charles withdrew a gun from the holster inside his jacket. Blue withdrew the one from the holster beneath his hoodie.

"Why are you armed?" Blue asked him.

"Because I was mugged last year, and I don't intend to let it happen again. Why are you?" Charles returned.

"Same reason," Blue lied, and the two men regarded each other with a wary, distrustful stare.

"Something is off about this whole situation," Charles said. "And I'm taking Jane with me." He drew her to him.

"She stays with me," Blue said, drawing her back.

Jane rolled her eyes. "For goodness sake, why don't we all get out of here before whoever did the shooting comes looking."

Blue and Charles nodded their agreement, though neither wanted to be the first to break eye contact. Sighing, Jane turned and began heading out of the alley, forcing them to jog to catch up with her. They flanked her, both of them so tall next to her that they looked like an M in motion. On the street, nothing appeared amiss, but Charles's car was toward the restaurant and Blue's was away from it. They went there, intending to drive around until they were certain they were in the clear.

"This is your car?" Charles asked, stopping short in front of Blue's Jaguar. He whistled. "The Smithsonian must pay better than my museum."

"I never said I work for the Smithsonian," Blue replied.

"Where do you work?" Charles asked.

"I never said," Blue said. They got into the car, locked the doors, and started to drive. Charles turned to the back seat to look at Jane.

"What exactly are you into, Janie?" he asked.

"Nothing, a bit of consulting work," she replied vaguely.

"Did it ever occur to you the source of your danger is also your driver?" Charles asked her.

"Hmm," Jane said, pretending to consider Blue. "Now that you mention it, he is a little shifty, what with the tattoos and all."

Blue smiled. "I thought we were past that."

"Maybe I'm coming full circle," Jane said.

Blue started to reply and stopped as his gaze slid to the mirror. "I think we have a tail."

Charles turned to look. "How can you be certain?"

"Because I saw that same red sedan before we arrived at the restaurant. It only followed us a couple of blocks then, so I didn't think much of it. But now it's back, and there's no reason for that." He accelerated, heading onto the freeway. "How well can you shoot?"

"I'll suffice," Charles replied. "How well can you drive?"

"I'll suffice," Blue said, flooring it to a hundred as he wove in and out of traffic.

"Hey, Independence Hall," Jane said, spying a sign for it.

"That's my little nerd history buff," Charles said, reaching behind to give her a pat on the knee.

No, that's MY *little nerd history buff,* Blue wanted to say. But he didn't because doing a hundred on the freeway wasn't exactly ideal conditions for posturing with a rival.

The red car kept pace for a while, close enough to be menacing, not close enough to tell who was behind the wheel. No shots were fired, and eventually Blue was able to shake them. They circled for a while before heading back toward the restaurant where they'd been, along with Charles's car.

The street was clear when they approached. The diner's window had been boarded up but otherwise there were no signs of the earlier shooting. Blue double parked beside Charles's car. Charles turned to the back seat, to Jane.

"Jane, get out of the car and come with me."

Blue turned toward the back also. "Jane, stay in the car, you're going with me."

"She's not safe with you," Charles said, turning his attention to Blue.

"She's still alive, isn't she?" Blue replied, facing Charles.

"But for how long? Look, I appreciate that you believe you have her best interest in mind, but you're up against armed men. What does a computer geek know about that?"

"As much as a museum geek, apparently," Blue replied.

"Jane, tell him you feel safer with me," Charles demanded, turning to face Jane again. But Jane couldn't reply because Jane was gone.

Blue threw the car into park and both men bolted from the car, searching for Jane. They found her a few yards away, doubled over by the edge of the alley. "Jane," Blue called while Charles called, "Janie."

Jane held up a hand, warding them away. "Stay over there," she called. Her voice sounded faint and she gripped the wall to keep herself upright.

"Are you hurt?" Blue asked, advancing on her anyway. When he reached her, she stood upright, pivoted, and practically fell into his arms.

"No, I'm sick."

Blue stopped short, his arms easing comfortingly around her. "You're sick?"

She nodded against his chest. "Can we go home?" she whispered.

"Sure, sweetheart," he soothed, trying hard to keep the smugness out of his tone. She had chosen him. True, she was sick and possibly delirious, but he would take it for whatever it was worth.

"I'll call you," Charles said as they passed, keeping a safe distance from her in case she was sick again. She nodded, not attempting to talk to him. Blue opened the car door for her and closed it once she was safely inside.

He started the car. Jane directed the air vents at her face, and he turned the air conditioner up a notch. His hand rested on her leg in what he hoped was a soothing gesture. "Do you often get sick like this?" he asked.

She shook her head; her eyes were closed.

"Do you think it's the flu?" he asked.

She shrugged. "Blue, please, I don't want to talk," she whispered, though she did rest her hand on his to soften any sting from her words. He clasped her hand, and she returned the gentle pressure of his touch.

They rode like that for a while until Blue's stomach began to roil and pitch. Suddenly he understood why Jane might be ill. They had eaten the same thing and, based on the poor condition of the restaurant, food poisoning was almost a certainty.

Now it was his turn to crank up the AC and point it at his face. He felt hot and cold all at once. When was the last time he'd thrown up? He couldn't remember, it had been so long. He had a cast-iron stomach, not prone to nausea or illness. But not now. Right now his stomach felt like a tiny airplane in high turbulence. Jane groaned, pressing her hand to her stomach.

"Can you pull over," she moaned.

Blue yanked the car to the side of the road, tossed it into park, and they both dashed out, getting simultaneously sick a yard away from each other on the side of the road. Thankfully they were both too immersed in their own misery to be grossed out by each other.

"Oh," Blue moaned, and Jane followed suit. They stumbled back to the car and leaned against it, too sick and weak to take the necessary steps to get back inside.

"Can you drive home?" Jane whispered. She was sprawled haphazardly on the car, her pale face pressed to the hood.

"It's only a few blocks," Blue said. He was in nearly the same position, only his face was pressed to the car's top, given his greater height advantage. The cool of the metal felt heavenly beneath his sweaty, overheated face.

"Can you?" she pressed.

"I honestly don't know," Blue said. "I'm going to need a minute."

"Blue," Jane groaned, pressing her hand to her stomach.

"Mm," he said, doing the same to his abdomen.

"You are never allowed to pick the restaurant again," she said.

"Agreed," he murmured before they ran to two new spots and got sick again.

CHAPTER 23

No one was awake by the time they made it home, but Blue woke his mother. What was the advantage of being home if his mommy didn't take care of them? And take care of them she did, setting them up at opposite ends of the couch with lined trash cans, sparkly lemon-lime soda, peppermints, and cool wash cloths for their foreheads. After taking turns in the bathroom a few more times, they finally stopped getting sick. They were even able to drink some of the soda and suck on the mints they'd been provided. Jane wanted to brush her teeth, but she was too weak. Eventually—wrung out, wasted, exhausted—they fell asleep.

Jane woke a few hours later, alarmed and confused. Where was she? She sat up, caught sight of Blue at the other end of the sofa, and it all came crashing back. She had gotten sick in front of a near stranger, one she found intensely attractive, had been tended to by his mother. Her stomach still felt weak and queasy, but more from lack of food than lingering illness. She sipped the lukewarm, now-flat soda and lay back down. She thought Blue was still asleep, but a moment later, he spoke.

"How do you feel?" he whispered.

"About as well as you do, I'd imagine," she said. The food poisoning had been brutal. "Sorry I shoved you out of my way that last trip to the bathroom."

"I had it coming, I was lingering," he said, pinching her toe. They shared a smile. "Sorry I took you on a date that almost killed you in multiple ways."

"Was that actually a date?" she asked.

"It was supposed to be," he said.

"At least it was memorable. I've never been on a date that started with a workout and charley horses, got shot at in the middle, and ended with food poisoning. Other guys are going to have a lot to live up to after this."

He tossed aside the blanket, crawled to her end of the couch, and forced her to make room for him as he took her in his arms. "I don't want there to be other guys, Jane."

She rested her head on his chest, returning his embrace. "I think we've been over this already."

"I don't like the conclusion we determined," Blue said.

"Tell me what's changed," Jane replied. "Can you live with not knowing things about me, secrets about my past and present?"

"Why did you leave the table again before the waitress arrived?" he blurted.

"To create a diversion to poison you. But clearly I messed it up and dosed both of us instead," Jane said.

He squeezed her. "The truth."

"Because ordering food at restaurants sends me into a panic spiral. The only thing worse for my social anxiety is making me talk on the phone or be in the spotlight in front of a large group of strangers," Jane said.

"Why didn't you tell me that instead of disappearing?" he asked.

"Do you tell people all your weirdly personal faults?" she asked.

"If it will help them realize I'm not a criminal," he said, wincing as his words registered. "I mean, not that I think you're a criminal, I don't, it's just…"

"It's just there are some lingering doubts in your mind you can't erase," Jane said.

"A bit," he admitted.

"Because I have no virtual footprint," she added.

"You're the only person I've ever met who doesn't. Literally, Jane, the only person in the known universe. I've run criminals who paint a clearer picture than you do."

"And it bothers you," she said.

"Yes," he bit out.

"There we go, back to square one."

"Just tell me," he begged.

"No."

"Even if it means we can't be together?" he asked.

She pressed her palms to his chest and shifted so she could see his face. "I guess what I need from you is a willingness to be together even though you don't have all the answers about me, not a desire to get all the answers in order to decide if you want to be with me. Does that make sense?"

"No," he stubbornly insisted.

"It makes sense to me," she said.

"Of course it does, you're a criminal mastermind. The cutest one ever." He gave her another squeeze, and she rested her head on his chest again, exhausted, depleted.

"You're kind of comfy for an overly curious, too tall computer geek," she said.

"That's because we have something. We fit, we have chemistry."

"I don't deny that," Jane agreed.

"There's only this one little obstacle standing in the way," he said.

"My stubborn insistence on getting to know each other like normal people?" she said.

"No, your stubborn insistence on keeping your past secret," he said.

"My past isn't a secret. I've already told you it was unusual, I was homeschooled, I grew up mostly in Africa, and I have two sisters. You know what my degree is, where I work, my dating history and room-mates. What else is there?"

"What about your dad? You won't talk about him."

She sighed. "My entire life has been defined by my dad's choices. I don't want it to be that way with you."

"I swear it won't affect the way I feel about you," he said.

"But it will. I guarantee it will, and we're not there yet. Someday you'll know everything, and maybe by then it won't matter. But right now it will matter, possibly a lot."

"Jane, you're so adorably stubborn, and if my esophagus and throat didn't feel as if they'd been dipped in battery acid, I would totally kiss you right now."

"And if I weren't dying for a toothbrush and a long, hot shower, I'd totally kiss you back," Jane replied. "But for now this is nice."

"Yes, it is," he agreed. They lay cuddled up on the couch, folded together in a cozy pose, despite their combined weakness and misery. Within a few minutes, they fell back asleep, waking again when Blue's phone rang.

He woke with a start and lunged for it. By the ringtone, he knew it was Ridge. He hadn't called to report the gunshot or the tail. Had his boss somehow caught wind? Was Blue about to be reamed?

With effort, he reached into his pocket, straining his long arms around Jane who ducked low to allow his hand access to his pocket. "Hello," Blue said, his voice scratchy from disuse and sickness.

There was a pause and then, "Did I wake you?"

Blue checked the time. It was ten in the morning. In Ridge's world, that was like sleeping until four in the afternoon and a definite strike against being a responsible employee or human being. "Rough night," Blue said.

"Anything I should be aware of?" Ridge said.

"Parts of it," Blue said. He closed his eyes and tried to take a deep breath, not an easy task when Jane was pillowed on his chest. Not that he was complaining. His fingers skimmed absently through her hair, and she snuggled into him, still half asleep.

"You can put it in your report," Ridge said.

Blue gripped the phone tighter. "What?" They did reports at the end of a mission, not in the middle.

"It's over. Ethan caught the middleman in Iraq. He's been smuggling the forgeries in and out of the country, shuttling the funds to and from the terror groups."

"But who's the forger?" Blue asked.

"We don't know yet, but with this guy out of the running, it doesn't matter."

"Is it safe for Jane?" Blue asked and she wriggled, blinking in confusion at the mention of her name.

"We'll keep an eye on her, but yes. The entire operation is essentially shutdown; there's nothing left to authenticate. Bring her home, and we'll work on a few long term security measures for her."

"Okay," Blue said.

Ridge paused. "You doing okay? You sound…not yourself."

"Food poisoning, but I'm fine," Blue assured him.

"Definitely leave that out of the report," Ridge said. They disconnected, and Blue tossed his phone onto the coffee table.

"It's over?" Jane asked.

"It's over," Blue affirmed. His hand smoothed the hair away from the back of her neck, and he felt suddenly as if he had known her for years instead of weeks. Had he ever been this comfortable with a woman, with anyone?

"How can it be over?" Jane asked. "Did they catch the forger?"

"They don't need to; we got the smuggler. He was the one with direct ties to the terror cell we've been chasing."

"But the forger's still out there," Jane said. "Still wreaking havoc on my industry."

"I know, and we're hopeful the guy we have in custody will point us in his direction. We'll keep working on it, along with a few other agencies. Either way, your part is finished. You're free."

"Yay," she said, albeit sadly.

They lay in quiet, comfortable silence a few minutes, and then Jane sat up. "I'm going to wash up, if you don't mind." Not waiting for an answer, she rolled off the couch and headed for the bathroom.

When she emerged, Blue took his turn in the shower. They ate a quiet, subdued breakfast of Cheerios. Blue's mother was back at work, his father was sleeping, and that was why they told themselves they were hushed. The truth was both were feeling a bit melancholy at the impending departure. Each thought somehow by the time the end came the other would have given in. Jane thought Blue would have given up his need to know her secrets while Blue believed Jane would have told him everything by now. The reality was that neither was willing or ready to give, and so they were at an impasse.

The drive back to DC was equally quiet, awkwardly so. They reached her apartment sooner than either of them wanted, but neither made a move to leave the car.

"I don't want this to be the end," Blue said.

"I think it's for the best," Jane countered. "Clean break, ending on a high note, no hard feelings, no baggage. That's so rare it's kind of a gift, you know?"

Blue blew out a breath. "Please don't marry the guy."

Jane didn't reply. She leaned over the seat, pressed her lips to his like a benediction, slipped out of the car, and disappeared inside.

CHAPTER 24

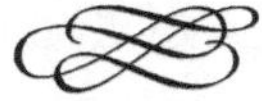

Six months later...

"You look so beautiful," Emily breathed, staring at Jane in the mirror as she stared at herself.

"Gorgeous," Nick added absently, as the apple he munched took up the main part of his focus.

"It's way too big for me," Jane said, fluffing helplessly at the wedding gown's long, white train.

"Of course it is," Emily agreed. "But you still look good."

"I'll say she does," Nick echoed. "Heartbreakingly so."

Jane rolled her eyes at him and returned her attention to Emily. "Tell me again why I'm wearing the dress if you're the one getting married."

"I needed to see it on someone else to make sure I like it."

"But you're way taller and curvier than I am," Jane said.

"It's not about that. It's about the feeling I get when I see it on someone. And I like the feeling. I think this one is a keeper," Emily said.

"What does it mean that you're taking longer to pick out a wedding dress than it did to meet and fall in love with your fiancé?" Jane asked.

"Don't poke at it, Janie. I'm happy," Emily pled.

"I'm not poking. Well, I am, but with love. I'm happy you're happy, but it doesn't mean I get to stop teasing you," Jane said.

"Never," Emily agreed. She sucked a sharp breath. "I can't believe I'm going to be married in two weeks."

"I can't believe I'm finally getting an actual bedroom in two weeks," Nick said, beaming. "I could have it now, if Jane would stop being stubborn."

Jane held up her phone and pushed a button. Taylor Swift's "We Are Never Ever Getting Back Together" began to play.

"Stop it," Nick said, covering his ears. Jane had refused his proposal as soon as she returned from Philadelphia. He had nearly cried—with relief. After some prodding, he confessed he had only proposed out of the blind panic her interest in Blue caused. But seeing as how she and Blue amounted to nothing, and she hadn't seen or heard from him in six months, Nick felt safe and secure once again. Annoyed by his proprietary certainty she wasn't going anywhere, Jane had put the song on her phone and played it every time he hinted they should be a couple again. She played it a lot, and it never ceased to annoy him.

"You're going to be the most beautiful bride in the universe," Jane said, hugging Emily. "And I'm going to get all my weeping out now before the big day so it will be nothing but sunshine and rainbows."

"Me, too," Nick agreed, hugging them from Jane's other side.

"I know it seems like I'm breaking up the team, but you guys are going to get married someday, too," Emily said.

"I know we are," Nick said confidently.

"She meant to other people," Jane snapped.

"The more you fight it, the more I'm certain of your undying love," Nick said.

Jane reached for her phone.

"Jane, play that song again, and you're going to regret it," he threatened.

She played the song. He let go of Emily and lunged for her. Jane gave a strangled scream of alarm, not for herself, but for Emily's wedding dress. "No," she said, dodging away from him. He caught her from behind, and the front door flew open.

In one fluid motion, Jane pivoted out of Nick's embrace, picked up a wooden kitchen chair, and bashed it into the intruder's body. Blue dropped to the ground, clutching his arm. "Ouch, Jane, *ouch*. Why? Why a chair? Why not a pillow?"

Jane stood over him, breathing hard, chair still held aloft. "Don't you ever knock?"

"You screamed." His eyes scanned her up and down, reminding her she still wore Emily's wedding dress and held a chair over his head. "Are you going to have that altered? You're swimming in it."

Jane set the chair down without answering. She scanned the dress for signs of wear and tear, breathing a sigh of relief when she found nothing. The dress was still perfect and perfectly white. "I need to take this off."

"I'll help," Nick volunteered, reaching for the back of the dress.

Jane held her phone aloft, warning him away.

"I swear, Jane, do it and I will break off every one of your delightful little fingers and bake them in a pie," he threatened.

"You're too lazy to make a pie," Jane returned.

"I'll help with the dress," Emily volunteered, herding Jane into the back bedroom to help remove the heavy, cumbersome dress.

"What is he doing here?" Jane whispered, standing still with her arms over her head while Emily unzipped her and lifted the dress over her head.

"I don't know, but I think he's gotten cuter," Emily replied, also in a whisper. "Nick's probably out there drafting a new proposal right now."

"He's not allowed to come barging back into my life when I've been trying to get over him the last six months," Jane continued.

"And failing miserably," Emily added helpfully. She hung up the dress and tossed Jane her clothes when she remained rooted to the floor, staring dazedly into space.

"I don't want to go back out there. You go. Tell him I'm sick."

"He just saw you. Do you think he's going to believe you miraculously came down with the swine flu in the short time we've been away? Go see what he wants. You've got this."

Jane nodded dumbly and turned for the door. Emily grabbed the back of her bra and hailed her back. "You should probably put clothes on first, unless you're trying to send a whole different kind of message."

"Yeesh," Jane muttered, reaching for her pants with shaking hands. She slipped back into her shirt. "I'm going to cry."

Emily pinched her arm, hard. The only thing that made Jane not cry was anything that should make her cry. Against pain, fear, and heartache she was stoic, a champ. But tiny frustrations and disappointments seemed hardwired to her tear ducts.

"Thanks," Jane said, taking another steadying breath. She reached for the door and paused again. "He has gotten cuter. What do you think he wants?"

"Go ask him," Emily urged, giving her a little shove forward.

"You're really not going to let this go until I do it, are you?" Jane said.

"No, and send Nick back here so he doesn't stand there like the unwanted interloper he is," Emily commanded.

"I think I might want him there. I need the buffer to remind me why men are bad and I want nothing to do with them, and no one does that better than Nick," Jane said.

"Good point," Emily agreed.

When Jane returned to the living room, Blue was now standing. He and Nick faced each other, as if they'd been having a conversation, but no one was talking when Jane entered the room.

"That took a bit, darling," Nick said. Jane tossed him a look, annoyed by his blatant and undeserved possessiveness.

"So," Blue said, drawing her attention to him.

"Not to be rude, but what are you doing here?" she asked.

"I need you."

"You…need me?" she echoed.

"I mean the team needs you. For work purposes."

"I thought that was over," she said.

"Nothing's ever really over," Blue said.

"Amen to that," Nick agreed, nudging Jane.

She reached for her phone and discovered she had left it in her bedroom. "I can't now. I have a busy couple of weeks coming up."

"I don't think you understand—I'm only asking as a formality. I'm here to bring you in."

"Are you telling me I don't have a choice over whether or not I work with you?" she said.

"Not when it's a matter of life and death," he replied.

"Does this have anything to do with your da…" Nick began, but Jane cut him off.

"No, I'll explain when it's over," Jane promised.

"Probably not because it will still be classified," Blue added. "You should pack some things. It might be a while."

"I don't like this," Jane said.

"You can tell me all about it in the car," Blue said. "Do you need help with the packing?" he added when she remained rooted to the spot.

"No." She blinked at him, her mind slowly coming to terms with two things: first he was standing in her living room asking her to come with him. Again. Second, despite trying hard to put him out of her mind and get over him in the intervening six months since she'd last seen him, she was ridiculously and overtly in love with him. Also, she was staring at him or, rather, she was staring at his mouth.

"Pack," the mouth said, and she finally tore her gaze away and headed for her bedroom.

Once there, she closed the door and leaned against it, feeling slightly woozy. "What did he want?" Emily whispered.

"He needs me."

"He needs you?" Emily asked hopefully.

"For a work thing. Consulting. I have to pack things."

"Can't move away from the door, can you?" Emily guessed.

"Not if I want to stay upright." She bent over and released a puff of air. "How am I going to do this, Em? How am I going to see him again and pretend it means nothing and then say goodbye?"

"Maybe you won't. Maybe the work thing is a cover. Maybe he just wants to see you," Emily suggested helpfully.

"If that's the case, where's he been the last six months?" Jane stood upright, shaking her head. "No, I was always the instigator there, always more into it than he was. But not this time. I'm going to play it cool, keep myself in check." Someone knocked on the door behind her. Jane yelped, stumbled forward, and fell into a heap on the floor before sitting up on all fours like a dog.

"Starting now, you mean," Emily asked.

"That didn't count. Starting now, I'm going to be cool," Jane said, using the bed to pull herself back to a standing position. "Who is it?"

"Jane, not to bug you, but kind of time sensitive here," Blue called.

"Yes, I'm coming." Turning to Emily she added, "Help me."

"You get your toiletries, I'll gather your clothes," Emily said, springing into action. She tossed Jane's suitcase onto the bed and began gathering things to put into it while Jane whipped open the door and ran face first into Blue who was still on the other side.

"Okay?" he asked, grasping her biceps to keep her upright.

"Nose print," Jane blurted.

"No," Blue replied.

"I meant I think I left a nose print on your chest when I bounced off it," Jane explained.

"I knew what you meant, and you're good, no nose print."

"Toiletries?" Jane said, and why it came out like a question she had no idea.

"Bathroom," he replied, letting her go and sidestepping out of her way.

"I see you downloaded the most current version of the Jane nervously awkward translation app," Emily commented.

"Virus free," Blue replied, and Emily chuckled.

"How long am I packing her for?" she asked.

"Three days, maybe?" Blue guessed, leaning in the doorway to watch. "Can I help?"

"I'm good, thanks," Emily said.

"I can't think of one person I would trust to pack my clothes for me," he remarked.

"Jane and I go back a long way," Emily said. "She's extra special to me."

"I know the feeling," he said, but he sounded a bit melancholy. Emily bit her tongue against the urge to interfere. Jane returned with her toiletries, double checked what Emily had packed, zipped the suitcase and pulled it off the bed.

"I love you," Jane said. Unfortunately the motion of twisting her suitcase off the bed now meant she was facing Blue when she spoke. He stared at her, blinking without expression. "Emily," she added, swiveling to face her friend. "Love you." *Kill me now*, she mouthed.

Emily laughed, scurried over the bed, and drew Jane into a comforting hug. "Love you, too. Be back in two weeks or I'll hunt you down like a dog in the street."

"I positively would not miss what's coming, no matter what," Jane promised. She kissed Emily's cheek, gave her one final squeeze, and let her go.

Blue picked up her suitcase and carried it to the living room where they were waylaid by Nick who scooped Jane into his embrace and kissed her full on the lips, something he hadn't done since before the last time they broke up well over a year ago. She shoved away from him, shell shocked and dumfounded, but in notorious Nick fashion, he grinned at her, well pleased with himself. "Goodbye, darling. I love you so. Do be careful." To Blue he added. "Take good care of my girl."

Jane came to and reached for her phone, but Nick preempted her, snatching it out of her fingers. "Let me get that for you." He turned it off and handed it back to her before she could play what had become their theme song in life. With a little smack on her bottom, he shoved her toward the door. Blue preceded her out, suitcase in hand. Jane hung back, poking her head inside the door to speak to Nick.

"I'm going to kill you, slowly and painfully," she promised.

"Something to look forward to then," he said. He kissed his fingers and tossed her a wave. Aggravated beyond reason, she slammed the door and stalked away.

CHAPTER 25

The elevator ride was unbearable. Neither Jane nor Blue seemed to know what to say to each other, and so they stood side by side in heavy silence. The only saving grace was that Jane lived on the fourth floor, and the time was blessedly short. Once out of the elevator, it seemed easier to breathe, if not easier to talk.

Blue drove his own car. He hauled Jane's suitcase into the trunk, and then they started to drive. "How have you been?" he asked after he was safely on the road.

"Well," Jane assured him, "Really well." He did not need to know about the few weeks of misery she'd suffered after his departure. Eventually she was able to shove her sadness down into a pit, one so deep it rarely surfaced anymore. "And you?"

"Great," he said, smiling.

Jane turned to stare out the window, trying not the let the word lance her heart. Of course he had been great. He had likely gotten over her so quickly and easily it was as if they never met, at least in his heart and mind. For Jane, who tended to love in an everlasting sort of way, it was likely she would never get over him completely. The only way she had been able to get over Nick was because he repeatedly cheated on her and broke her heart, and even then she wasn't able to let go of him completely, keeping him not only in her life but also in her apartment. After Emily moved out, it would be the two of them. They would likely be those old people who stayed single but never got back together, bickering roommates forever, like Mathew and Marilla Cuthbert. Maybe someday they would adopt a redheaded orphan and bicker over her upbringing, buy a farm on Prince Edward Island, make it official. The prospect made her stomach lurch. She wanted more than a love/hate relationship with her ex.

"I forgot how still you get," Blue noted.

Jane turned to look at him and saw him regarding her with a look of warm affection. Her heart turned over. "I forgot…" she began but petered out before she could continue. *I forgot how much being with you affects me, how deep my attraction to you goes, how much I like you, how right it feels when we're together.* "My lip balm," she continued lamely. "I left it on my nightstand."

"You can have some of mine," he said, his gaze dropping to her lips before returning to the road.

Jane turned to stare out the window again, not sure what to do with that statement.

"I guess congratulations are in order," he said a few minutes later.

She bestowed her attention on him again. "Hmm?"

"On your wedding. Nick said you two are getting married in two weeks," Blue said.

She blinked at him. "Nick said what?"

"I asked him when the wedding was. He said two weeks."

Jane pressed her lips together. Nick most assuredly knew what Blue had assumed when he saw her wearing Emily's wedding dress. She could almost hear his words when she confronted him about it. *What? I never said you and I were getting married. I simply went along with his assumption.* Then he would grin at her in aggravating Nick fashion, assuring she wouldn't actually be able to maintain her irritation with him. She whipped out her phone and fired off a text to him, pausing to turn on her phone again after he'd turned it off.

You are seriously one messed up individual, and I am ridiculously angry with you.

He replied a minute later. *I did it for you, to give you a security net and ratchet down the awkward tension. You're welcome.*

He hadn't done it for her, she knew. He had done it for his own jealously and orneriness. But she would take it for the gift it was and use it as a buffer between her and Blue. Goodness knew she had no ability to resist him on her own.

"Thank you."

"Where's your ring?" Blue asked, touching her left hand.

"In a box on Nick's nightstand." That part was true. After she refused his proposal, Nick told her he would leave the box by his bed (meaning her couch) for whenever they decided to get together and "make it official." That was exactly the moment when Jane downloaded the Taylor Swift song and began playing it on repeat. She would never get desperate enough to take Nick's sloppy, backhanded proposal. She might not be someone's first choice, but she was no one's leftovers. "Are you seeing anyone?"

He returned both hands to the wheel. "I've been seeing a lot of people. No one in particular, and no one on repeat."

"Hmm." Hearing him answer her question had given her an excuse to look at him. She stared at his profile and realized she had forgotten none of it. Over the last few months she had been able to conjure his face as easily as if he were standing beside her. In a ridiculously short time it had become much beloved by her, like a favorite painting. They reached a stoplight and he faced her, returning her frank stare, a small smile playing on his lips.

"I missed you, Jane," he said and someone behind them honked. Blue faced forward again and accelerated through the green light.

"I missed you, too," Jane admitted, forcing her eyes away from him as she faced forward.

"Really? In the midst of getting engaged and planning a wedding you found time to miss me?" he asked, a hint of bitterness creeping into his tone.

"I…" Jane began, but didn't know how to continue. Blast Nick and his lie, and blast her weakness for going along with it.

"Never mind, we're here," Blue said, holding his credentials aloft to the security guard who oversaw the agency's parking lot. He parked and she reached for her door, but he held her back. "One more thing I want to tell you before we go in."

She turned curiously to him.

"I sold your app."

She blinked at him. "My app?"

"The translator for social awkwardness. They loved it, it's been selling like hotcakes."

She gasped, pressing her hands to her mouth in excitement. "You're joking."

He shook his head, grinning. "I'm not, it's been selling better than Threeple. I'm thinking of buying another Jag, one for the weekends. I'll get you one, too. What's your favorite color?"

"I don't want a Jag, but I do want to see the app."

He pulled out his phone, pressed a button, and handed it over. It featured a quick response for every conceivable social setting, as well as conscious relaxation exercises and reminders. "This is fantastic," she said.

"Do you want to see your Easter egg?" he asked.

She looked up and froze. He was very close to her face, mere inches away. She could smell him now, and the pheromones were a powerful reminder of her attraction to him, as if she needed one. She nodded. He took the phone back, his fingers brushing hers as they made the pass. He pressed a button and turned the phone toward her. With effort, she settled her eyes back on the device in time to see a cartoon drawing of what was obviously the two of them on his screen. Jane sat on a bench, Blue knelt in front of her, and she took his face in her hands and kissed him. The cheesesteak shop was behind them.

"Our first kiss," she muttered, her heart somersaulting around her chest. He nodded. "I love it, it's perfect. Congratulations." Unbidden, her arms slid around him, hugging him.

He hugged her in return, an innocent hug of friendship. Or at least that was how it started out. Eventually he swallowed convulsively and dropped his head, inhaling her hair. "Jane," he whispered, and his phone buzzed with a text. He froze.

"Work?" she guessed.

"They'll be wondering where we are. I was supposed to retrieve you poste haste."

They pulled apart. "Let's go then," Jane said, stepping from the car and heading toward the building before her.

They were at Blue's office. Jane had only been there once before, so she was still fascinated by the layers of security. She peered curiously at everything, intrigued by the rare glimpse into the underbelly of spy life. If one didn't know what it was, it would have appeared like any other corporate office with worker bees scurrying to and from cubicles.

After they were through the many layers of security, including retina scans for both of them, they stepped onto an elevator that took them up multiple levels to a secure conference room. Jane was intent, taking it all in, staring at the elevator keypad as she tried to envision what was on all the other floors. It was a bit like The Ministry of Magic in Harry Potter, each floor providing a different function. Blue's floor was on the twelfth level, high up but not the top. The secure conference room was on the fifteenth. There were twenty floors. What was on the top?

"I love that look on your face when you're curious," Blue noted, and Jane realized he'd been watching her for some time.

"The nerd look?" she guessed.

He nodded, smiling. "You should patent it."

"I don't think there's a big market," Jane replied.

"I'd buy it," he said, his fingers brushing hers. There was something different about him, but Jane couldn't pinpoint what it was. He seemed more intent, in some way more resolved. Before she could puzzle over it, the elevator doors opened and the rest of his team was there—Ridge, Maggie, Ellen, Babs, and Ethan. And they all stared at Jane and Blue.

Jane froze, a deer in headlights. "I'm going to need your app," she whispered. It was her worst nightmare, being the center of attention among a group of strangers who all knew each other. Though she wasn't exactly a stranger, a fact proved when Ridge offered her a friendly smile and greeting and his wife, Maggie, stepped forward to hug her.

"Did Blue warn you Maggie's a hugger?" Ridge asked.

"Eventually you stop fighting it and begin to enjoy it," Babs promised as Jane awkwardly returned Maggie's hug. Whether it was the hug or the warm welcome, her tension dissipated enough not to make her blurt something stupid or offensive.

"Hi," she said, smiling like a normal person as she added a little wave for the group.

"I think we're all here," Ridge said. "Let's get started." He led the way to the conference room and held the door for everyone as they filed past him. Once seated, he ascended to the front of the room and picked up a remote.

"Thanks for agreeing to meet with us on such short notice, Jane," Ridge said.

"No problem," Jane said, though she still wasn't sure what she was doing there.

"I'm sure Blue explained our situation," Ridge said.

"Eh, no," Blue replied.

"Why not, Blue? What were you doing instead?" Ethan prodded, grinning in a way that reminded Jane strongly of Nick. Across from them, Maggie reached for her phone and fired off a text. Blue's phone buzzed. He picked it up, snickered, and shook his head.

"Right, okay, then let me get you caught up. After we captured the smuggler, we were able to apprehend the terror cell he'd been working with. Some things were prevented, and it was a happy ending all around, except we were never able to find the forger. Our smuggler blabbed a lot, but the forger had been careful, covering tracks and leaving blinds and bluffs that, frankly, have kept us on a wild goose chase all this time. Things have been quiet until two days ago. Another transaction was made, this time with the proceeds going to a new terror cell. We've revised our earlier opinion and now believe the forger is actually the mastermind, and not merely a pawn in the scheme. We intercepted a picture of the artifact." Ridge clicked a button on the remote and a canopic jar sprang to life on the screen. Jane stood and walked forward to inspect it, tilting her head.

"This one's a fake," she declared after only a few minutes of looking at the picture.

"You can tell this easily and from a picture?" Ridge asked.

"Definitely. And this was not done by the same forger as before. This work is sloppy, amateurish. You would only need the barest knowledge of the field to be able to spot the ineptness of this work," she said.

"That's our problem," Ridge said. "You're the second person to tell us that information, but it complicates things for us. The original forger is still the one driving the sales, still the one pumping money into our terror cell. Why he's brought on an amateur is what has us baffled."

"I think it might be because of me," Jane said. She perched on the edge of the table, staring at the picture on the screen.

"How so?" Ridge asked. He crossed his arms over his chest, awaiting her answer. It was easy to forget the other people in the room, to pretend they were the only two there having a discussion. The topic was familiar and comfortable to Jane, bypassing her normal social anxiety triggers.

"He or she knows the fakes are being authenticated, that I'm looking into them, keeping an eye on the market. Last time he ordered my kidnapping, and his smuggler was caught before things could advance further. Maybe this time he reached out for help to flood the market, to keep me so busy I don't have enough time to authenticate everything. That way the sophisticated fakes can slip through unnoticed, thereby covering his tracks."

"That's what we thought, too. It's why we brought you back. With your agreement, Jane, we need you to help us flush him out," Ridge said.

"What did you have in mind?" Jane asked.

Ridge smiled. To Jane it looked a little calculated. "How would you feel about becoming a full fledged spy?"

CHAPTER 26

"Jane, are you sure you're okay with this?" Blue asked. They sat in his office, on differing sides of his desk, discussing their upcoming assignment.

"Are you joking? Outside of Indiana Jones, how often does an anthropologist get to do anything remotely this exciting?" Jane asked.

"We're going to be observed and covered. The danger is low," he assured her.

"Kind of harshing my buzz here," she said, pinching an eggroll with her chopsticks. "Let me have my secret agent moment in the sun."

"Well, there is some danger," he said. "Things could go south at any moment when you're in the field."

"Stop it, you're turning me on," Jane said.

"Just trying to bring you up to my level," Blue said, smiling.

"Who says I'm not already there?" Jane asked, reaching for a bite of noodle from his Chinese takeout container. She had picked the restaurant this time, thanks to his inability to be trusted with such a task.

"Despite your words to the contrary, you don't sound a hundred percent convinced. Do you not want to do it? I'll talk to Ridge, you don't have to."

"I want to, I swear," she said.

"Then what is it? What's bothering you?" he asked.

"It's really stupid. I'm embarrassed to tell you."

"Sweetheart, we've puked in tandem; our embarrassment days are over forever after that."

"You have a point there," Jane said. She took a breath. "I kind of wish I looked and felt more like a spy. I mean, we're going to this cool hacker bar to meet a possible forger and international terrorist, and I'm going to walk in like this." She spread her hands wide, indicating herself.

"What's wrong with how you look? I *like* how you look. You're adorable."

"Thank you, but I don't want to be adorable. I want to be dangerous and exciting and like the type of person who would show up at an underground hacker bar for an illicit meeting with a terrorist."

Blue leaned forward on his elbows, regarding her intently. "You know, we brought you on for your expertise of the subject, not because you look like a hardened criminal."

Jane blushed. "I know, I'm doing the girl thing where I feel insecure and overthink it. Never mind, I told you it was stupid. I'll show up in my regular black pants and gray sweater, and it will be fine."

"Maybe not," Blue said.

"You want me to show up naked?" she countered and his elbow slipped, causing his head to plummet a few inches before he righted himself.

"Geez, warn a guy before you start talking about yourself in the nude. While I would be totally fine with that prospect, I was thinking of something else, of someone who can make you look exactly the way you want to look."

"You have an ace up your sleeve?" she asked. "Some kind of super spy costumer?"

"No, I don't have an ace. I have an Amelia."

"Huh?" she said.

"Give me a minute. And don't eat all my noodles." He stood, pulled his phone from his pocket, and stepped out of the office, pushing a button as he left.

Amelia answered on the first ring.

"Hey, baby bear. Remember how you owe me about a thousand favors?" Blue began.

"Who is this?" Amelia asked, an unusually high amount of mischief in her tone.

"This is the guy who, with one push of a button, can turn your credit rating to yesterday's oatmeal."

"Oh, Blue, right. How's it going?"

"Super, and I need to call in a few favors."

"If you need me to kill someone for you, I'm afraid you've got the wrong spouse on the line," she said.

"I have someone who needs a makeover, and Ethan really stinks at those," he said.

"Fun. Who is it?"

"Her name is Jane. She needs to go less Ann Taylor and more Daft Punk, pronto."

"Double fun. I take it this is time sensitive," Amelia said.

"Tomorrow, if possible."

"I can squeeze you in after the salon closes, if that works."

"That works perfectly," Blue said.

"One condition," Amelia said.

"Condition? I don't remember adding a condition when you were stranded in Africa and in need of a passport," Blue said.

"Only because you didn't think of it," Amelia replied. "When you show up at the salon tomorrow, I expect you to be unshaved."

"I'll let Jane know."

"Not Jane. You. Don't shave in the morning or the deal's off," she said.

"Why?"

"You're going to have to trust me."

He looked around and lowered his voice. "Look, I have to warn you about Jane. She's not going to be easy. She's…really entrenched in her ultra-conservative style. You're going to have a hard time making her…"

"Let me interrupt you right there. I'm not going to have a hard time because you're vastly underestimating my abilities. See you tomorrow. Don't shave."

"You're a weird child," he said, but she'd already disconnected.

❦

The next day was spent planning and in meetings, making sure Jane was comfortable with the plan and well prepared to carry it out. Blue had set up a meeting with the hackers who represented the forger by going on the dark web and pretending to be an interested buyer. Jane would be going to authenticate the sale and ID the forger's work. The rest of the team would be listening in and providing cover, should the need arise. Blue would likewise be armed. He was trying to project a confident image, but, like Jane, he had never actually been needed in the field before. He was usually the one in the trailer running information behind the scenes.

Finally the day ended, and it was time to see Amelia.

Jane was nervous, but there was nothing new about that. Blue was cagey about where he was taking her, and when they showed up at a swanky salon in the nice part of town, her anxiety didn't back down.

"Um," she said.

"Amelia's going to fix you up," he said.

"Who is Amelia?" she asked. Blue kept referring to her as if Jane should have any idea who she was.

"Maggie's sister."

Jane rolled her eyes. Great. Just what she needed, another paragon of perfection. Did Blue have a thing for the sister, too? They parked and Blue held the door for her. They hadn't had much time alone together during the day. Now that it was just the two of them, the tension was back full force.

They reached the door of the salon. Blue put his hand on the door, but before he opened it, he leaned down and whispered in Jane's ear. "Just so we're clear, I'm a huge fan of the before."

Jane smiled up at him, her heart beating triple time. "And I yours," she said, then closed her eyes and shook her head. Why did the awkwardness have to come pouring out of her at the most inopportune times? Blue laughed and touched his finger to the end of her nose before opening the door and ushering her inside.

"Jane, hi, welcome." A blond woman who bore a strong resemblance to Maggie came forward and warmly shook Jane's hand. While Maggie was fresh-faced and cute with a girl-next-door appeal, the sister was the intimidating sort of pretty that always made Jane feel dowdy by comparison. Here was a woman who had likely never burned her forehead curling unfortunately short bangs. "We're going to have fun today. I'm going to hand you off to Alma for a moment. She'll get you something to drink, massage your hands, and wash your hair. Meanwhile," she clasped Blue's arm, "you're coming with me." She turned and began dragging him away.

He glanced helplessly at Jane who gave him a shrug. If he was hoping for a rescue, he was looking in the wrong place. She was completely out of her element in this place.

Amelia dragged Blue to another room and let him go. "So," she said, circling him like a monkey looking for mites.

"What's happening? Do I pass muster, General?"

"No," Amelia said. She stopped in front of him, crossing her arms. "Here's the deal. You're in dire need of a makeover."

"Um, no," Blue said. He motioned to himself. "This is my look."

Amelia rolled her eyes. "You know what this look says? 'I'm a teenage gamer who hangs out at the skate park on the weekends. And sometimes, if my mom gives me money, I go out for crullers with my friends.'"

"But," he began.

"Shh," she put her finger to her lips and interrupted him. "Mommy's still talking." She rested her hands on his shoulders and stared solemnly into his eyes. "You are a grown man, a highly trained spy, a secret agent tasked with the world's biggest secrets. Isn't it time you looked the part instead of like a Tony Hawk fanboy?"

"What did you have in mind?" he asked, his tone wary. He picked up his t-shirt and began nervously twisting the ends of it.

"First we start with the hair."

He put his hand to his signature blue tresses. "No way."

She nodded. "Yes way. You're going to put yourself in my hands, and when it's over, you don't have to tell me how right I am. All you have to say is, 'Thank you, Amelia.'"

She led him to a chair, washed his hair, and mixed the color she'd selected for him. She would return him to what she guessed was his natural color, a sandy blond. If it wasn't his natural color, it should be. He had a perpetually sun kissed complexion, like a California surfer who'd spent too much time on the board. While his color set, she checked in with Jane.

Alma had just finished washing her hair. She sat nervously in Amelia's chair, staring at herself in the mirror. "So, Jane," she said, and the woman jumped. She hunkered down beside Jane, staring at their combined reflection in the mirror.

"Tell me about this style. How long have you had it?"

Jane looked like she feared there was a wrong answer. Amelia took her hand and began gently petting it, something she did with her more skittish clients to soothe them. Jane returned her attention to her reflection in the mirror, surveying her harsh, chin-length bob. "Since I was fifteen. I lived in Africa and went through a big Egyptian phase. I thought it would make me seem more like Cleopatra."

"Cleopatra," Amelia said, tipping her head. "Interesting. Let me ask you another question. Do you ever feel like everyone in life is having an adventure but you?"

Jane nodded, her eyes filling with tears.

"Are you ready to change that?"

She nodded again, blinking hard to clear her eyes.

"Well, then, here we go." Amelia picked up her scissors and got to work.

Ninety minutes later, she returned to Blue. His hair was done, and it looked as amazing as she knew it would. She had colored the blue out of it and left it long on top, parting it on the top and slicking it to the side in an imitation of 1940's movie star glam. The day-old stubble on his cheeks gave his face more definition. Now it was time for the rest of him. She handed him a white dress shirt and a pair of pants.

"New clothes, too?" he asked, sounding much less disdainful than when he'd walked in nearly two hours ago.

"Trust me yet?" she asked and smiled when he reached for the clothes without comment. She left him and went to Jane who, like Blue, stood staring at herself in a full-length mirror.

"Is this really me?" she whispered.

"One hundred percent," Amelia said. "Except that stripe in your hair. It's temporary, but I can make it permanent, if you want."

"Maybe," Jane whispered, touching the blue stripe in her hair. Amelia had given her a modified pixie cut, leaving one long chunk that draped coquettishly over her forehead. That chunk of hair was now blue. Likewise Jane's makeup was completely over the top, yet still somehow worked. Amelia had done an exaggerated cat's eye on her, swirling the outer edges and dotting them with a heart on each side of Jane's temple. Her lipstick was bright pink but not gaudy or garish. Instead Jane looked somewhere between punk and adorable, and she kind of loved it.

"Jane, do you know how to tie a man's tie?"

"Yes, why?"

"Because Blue's going to need a teacher. Come with me." Amelia took her hand and led her next door where Blue stood in the center of the room. Or at least she thought it was Blue. It might easily have been a GQ model. He was polished, put together, well-tailored, and blond.

"Whoa," Jane whispered, taking in the sight of him.

His eyes brushed over her with no recognition. They fell to the door behind her, then to Amelia. "Is Jane almost done?"

Beaming now, Amelia put her arm around Jane and drew her front and center. "Jane Dunbar, may I introduce Blue Bishop?" She gave

Jane a little push. Jane stumbled, causing Blue to put out his hands to catch her. He grasped her hands and drew her closer, inspecting her as if she were a foreign object.

"Jane?" he whispered. "Is this the real Jane or did you kill her and make a replica?"

"Turns out this one was in there all along," Amelia said. "Oh, hey, I almost forgot. I have one more thing for you." She held up a tie, handing it to Blue.

"Uh, I don't know how to tie this," he said.

Amelia nudged Jane. "I do," Jane said softly. She took the tie, shook it out, and stood on her toes to slip it around Blue's neck.

"How do you know how to tie a man's tie?" he asked.

Her eyes met his. Was that a hint of jealousy in his tone or was it her imagination? "My dad."

"Ah," he said. "Look at you with the sleeve tats." He touched her arms where she wore literal sleeves with pictures of tattoos on them. Over that, Amelia had put a leather bustier atop a leather skirt. She looked punk but still with an air of sweetness. Now that he saw the change, he realized he wouldn't have been able to stand it if she looked hard.

"A blue tie," Jane said, smoothing it flat after she finished tying it. "Nice touch." Her eyes met Blue's again. "You look rather spectacular."

"Yeah?" he asked, smiling.

She nodded. Her hands seemed to have a mind of their own, first smoothing over his chest and then down his arms, ending at his hands where they clasped fingers.

"You're possibly the only person who could wear a leather bustier and still look innocent," he said. "I love the hair. So adorable." His fingers brushed the ends of her barely there pixie cut.

"Thank you. Do you think we'll fit at the place we're going?" she asked.

"I think we fit perfectly," he said, smiling as he swung their joined hands between them.

Jane inched closer, pressing her body lightly to his. "It's been a long six months, Blue."

"The longest," he agreed. His hands let go of hers and rested lightly on her hips. "Jane…" His phone buzzed. They froze.

"Work?" she guessed.

"I'd say they're probably wondering where we are," he said.

"I guess we'd better go," she said.

"Yes." He let her go, clasped her hand, and led her back to the main portion of the salon where Amelia was cleaning her station. He cleared his throat. Amelia looked up at him with an expectant smile.

"Thank you, Amelia," he said.

"Are we even?" Amelia asked.

"All debts are paid and then some," he replied.

"Well then you're welcome, Papa Bear. PS. Let me know how the night turns out."

"It's classified," he told her.

"Not the parts I want to hear," she said, tossing them a wink and a wave before returning to her work.

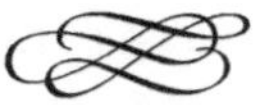

CHAPTER 27

No one recognized them. They showed up at the rendezvous point on time, a broken down warehouse two blocks from the underground hacker bar. Blue held the door for Jane, and they walked in side by side.

"I'm sorry, this building is closed," Ridge said almost absently before dropping whatever was in his hands and doing an almost comedic double take. Maggie and Babs stared at them, mouths agape. Only Ethan maintained the ability to speak.

"You've been to see Amelia," he noted.

"He knows Amelia?" Jane whispered.

"I hope so, he's married to her," Blue replied.

"Secretly married, Blue, *secretly*," Ethan reminded him.

"It's okay, she's one of us," Blue said.

"I guess that's true," Ethan said, shrugging as he turned his back to them and resumed whatever conversation he and Ridge had been having.

"Your hair's not blue," Maggie blurted, staring at Blue's head.

"But look, Jane's is. That's so cute," Babs said, linking arms with Maggie as they stared at Jane and Blue.

"Aw," Maggie said. "Oh, his tie is blue. My sister is a genius."

"Seriously, you guys look like you should be on the cover of a magazine," Babs agreed. "Like *Steampunk Monthly* or something."

"Or, I don't know, working?" Ridge suggested, slipping his arm around Maggie and giving her a squeeze.

"We're trying. Not our fault everyone is gawking," Blue said.

"But you're so adorable, Blue," Ethan said, pinching his cheek.

"That's it, you're getting hacked. Good luck getting into your car, building, credit cards, or bank account, *Becket,*" Blue threatened.

"Good luck getting home alive, Bishop," Ethan countered.

"On second thought, I may have been a bit hasty," Blue recanted.

"That's my pal," Ethan said, patting his shoulder. "Now let me see your gun."

"This is so sudden; I barely know you," Blue replied.

Ethan held out his hand, waiting for the weapon. "Good luck, Jane."

"What are you talking about? Jane's getting married to another man in two weeks," Blue replied.

All heads swiveled to stare collectively at Jane who immediately panicked. "I'm not. Not. Not, not. Not."

"She means she's not comfortable being stared at like the main attraction at a freak show. Eyes on your own papers, people," Blue said, and everyone busied themselves not staring at Jane. "*Sorry,*" Blue mouthed to Jane.

"Not," Jane said once more, and he sputtered a laugh before Ridge grabbed everyone's attention.

"Ethan, the gun good?"

"Gun's good," Ethan replied, handing it back to Blue. "Don't shoot until you see the whites of their eyes."

"Really?" Blue said.

Ethan snorted. "No. By that time you're already dead."

"This is your first time mentoring someone, huh?" Blue said.

"You're not going to have to shoot anyone. That's what Maggie and I are for," Ethan assured him.

"Maggie?" Jane said, jumping slightly in surprise at the mention of the librarian's name.

"Maggie's going to be on the roof across the street with a sniper rifle," Ridge said then, noting Jane's reaction, turned to Blue. "You did tell her about Maggie, didn't you?"

"A few things," Blue said.

"Maggie and the gun are one," Babs interjected.

"They have a better relationship than she and Ridge do," Ellen added.

"That is not true. Is it?" Ridge asked Maggie.

"Of course not," Maggie assured him. "Although the gun doesn't snore."

"So the librarian is your sharpshooter," Jane clarified.

"You should see what the janitor can do," Blue said, and Jane wasn't sure if he was joking.

"She's never killed anyone, if it makes you feel better," Ethan said, flicking Maggie's hair.

"Why are you so obsessed with that?" Maggie asked, punching him in the bicep.

"It's a brother's prerogative," he assured her.

"Well, brother, if your aim was as good as mine, you wouldn't have to take the kill shot, either," Maggie said.

"Ouch, my eyes and my ears hurt after witnessing that burn," Ellen said, covering her eyes with her hands.

"I'm telling Amelia you said hurtful things to me," Ethan threatened.

"I'm telling my parents you married their baby in a shady African ceremony," Maggie returned.

"It wasn't shady; it was rainy," Ethan countered.

"Is anyone pretending we're here to work?" Ridge asked.

"Uh-oh, Dad's mad," Blue whispered in a loud aside.

"Speaking of dads, Jane, can I have a word please?" Ridge said. They walked to the back of the building, well out of earshot for a while, and had a conference together.

"What's that about?" Ethan asked Blue.

"I think her dad is some kind of international super criminal or something," Blue said. "I told Ridge what I suspect, and he said he'd have a word with her about it."

"You don't know who he is or what he does?" Ethan said.

"She won't say," Blue replied.

"Huh. I guess that explains it," Ethan said.

"Explains what?"

"Why she's so, you know, unfazed by all of this. Almost get kidnapped and murdered? Fine. Get involved in trying to take down a terrorist ring? Okey-dokey. Not a lot of people would be so easygoing and comfortable with our world. Something to consider, my son. And there's your mentoring," Ethan said, tapping his temple.

"Did you hear the part about her marrying another man in two weeks?" Blue returned.

"Did you see her face when you brought that up?" Ethan parried.

"No. What was it doing?" Blue asked, but too late because Jane returned. "Everything okay?" he asked her instead.

"Fine," she said, smiling serenely.

"You know, Jane," Ethan began, "most people aren't that calm after a private conference with our boss."

"Really?" Jane said, her glance resting questioningly on Ridge. "He seems easygoing and gentle to me."

"I had to wear a diaper for the first year I knew him," Blue said.

"Me too," Ethan agreed.

"Hmm, I don't get it," Jane said.

"Keep her," Ethan whispered.

"Working on it," Blue replied.

They went over the plan a final time. Maggie and Ethan left to get in place, and then it was Blue and Jane's turn.

"Ready?" he asked.

"Sure," she replied. "Are you?"

"Definitely," he said. He clasped her hand and led the way two blocks to the secret hacker bar. It looked like any other abandoned, decrepit building on the block. If one didn't know better, it would be easy to walk right by the graffiti covered outside. But Blue stopped, reached behind the door, and pulled out a keyboard.

"You have to hack your way in," he explained at Jane's questioning glance. He typed furiously for a moment, and then the door swung open.

"So cool," Jane breathed. He clasped her hand and led the way inside. It wasn't her imagination that the crowded bar seemed to come to a standstill as all eyes were on them. "Why is everyone staring at us?"

"I had to use my hacker name to get in. After the Department of Defense thing, it's kind of infamous," he explained in a whisper.

"What's your hacker name?" Jane asked, intrigued.

"Cyan," he replied.

"Synonym for Blue. Cute," she said.

"Me or the name?" he asked, glancing down at her with a smile.

"Both," she replied, returning the smile. "If it's a hacker bar, how can Ethan get in?"

"He's already in."

She scanned the bar but didn't see him. "Where?"

Blue rolled his eyes skyward. Jane followed his glance and saw oversized heating ducts above them. "So cool," she breathed.

"Yeah, it kind of is," Blue agreed.

Blue led her to the back of the room where two men sat in a booth. Jane braced herself in case it was someone she recognized from the museum world, but the men were completely unfamiliar to her. Not so to Blue.

"Cyan, never thought I'd see you in person," the first one said.

"I feel like asking for your autograph," the second said. "Maybe I'll get it tattooed somewhere in binary."

"Cracker Jack, Nuthatch," Blue greeted them. "This is my..." he regarded Jane. She braced herself to hear what he would call her this time. Last time he had stumbled over "colleague." "Jane. This is my Jane." He took her hand, winding their fingers together. "You have a package for us?"

"You have Bitcoins for us?" the one called Nuthatch asked.

"Only if the package is good," Blue said.

"It's good," Cracker Jack was quick to assure him.

"We'll see," Blue said.

Nuthatch produced a box from beside him and set it on the table. Jane let go of Blue to reach for it. If it was a legitimate artifact, they were out of luck. She poked her head in the box, reached for the scarab, and withdrew it. It was good. It was very, very good. But it wasn't real. She gave Blue a slight shake of her head.

"No deal," Blue said.

"What?" Nuthatch exclaimed. "That's legit, Cyan. Seriously."

"Jane says otherwise," Blue replied.

"Who's she to know?" Cracker Jack asked.

"The preeminent expert in her field," Blue said. "I have to tell you, this does not make me happy. I hope I don't have to, hmm, retaliate." Nuthatch and Cracker Jack shuddered, and Jane repressed a smile. Her imagination ran wild imagining what two criminal hackers would find scary enough to be threatening from a fellow hacker.

"I swear, we thought it was good. He told us it was good."

"I want to see him," Jane interrupted, and the two men across the table looked at her.

"He doesn't want to be seen," Nuthatch said.

"Let me put it this way. I have a rather unlimited budget, but there's one caveat. It either has to be real or real enough to convince me. I want to talk to him and see if we can come to some kind of arrangement or agreement," Jane said.

Nuthatch and Cracker Jack regarded her, considering.

"Conjure him, and I'll give you a finder's fee worth your while," Blue promised.

Now the two men regarded each other. "Let me see what we can do," Nuthatch said, withdrawing his phone. He sent a text, waited for the answer, and nodded his assent. "He's coming. Cracker Jack has to let him in, he's not a hacker." Cracker Jack got up and headed for the door.

"So, Cyan, how'd you do it?" Nuthatch asked Blue.

"Do what?" Blue asked.

"Come on, you know what. How'd you crack the DoD?" Nuthatch said, leaning forward on his elbow, listening intently.

"Does a magician reveal his secrets?" Blue asked.

"Nobody's been able to do it since," Nuthatch said, shaking his head. Jane knew it was because Blue had taken over cyber security for the DoD, assuring no one would be able to hack it the same way he had. "Is it true you hacked the President's bank account?"

Blue pretended to lock his lips.

Nuthatch's attention was diverted behind them. "Here he comes."

Blue and Jane tried hard not to tense expectantly. Cracker Jack and another man slid into the booth across from them, and all of Jane's pretense slid away as recognition hit.

CHAPTER 28

"Nick," Jane exclaimed.

He seemed equally as dumbfounded to see her. "Janie. You cut your hair. I love it."

Jane's shock wore off, quickly replaced by anger. She leapt over the table, grabbed his shirt, and dragged him closer. "What are you doing here, you exponential moron?"

"Maybe you want to take this outside," Nuthatch suggested. "If we get kicked out of here, it's going to take more than we're worth to work our way back in."

"Fine," Jane said. She scooted from the booth, grabbed Nick by the arm, and frog marched him outside.

"Ouch, what is your problem?" Nick asked, shaking free from her as soon as they were outside.

"What is my problem? What are you doing here?" Jane asked.

"Are you still mad about the other day?" Nick asked.

Jane grabbed both his biceps and shook him. "Answer the question. What are you doing here?"

"Some guys said you wanted to have a conversation," Nick said.

Jane's hands went slack. She stared at him. "Do you have any idea what you've stumbled into?"

"What?" Nick asked, smiling. His hand slipped up, reaching for her hair.

"Don't touch her," Blue said, stepping forward, his hand reaching for the gun inside his jacket.

"Or what?" Nick asked. "You going to arrest me?"

"Not me," Blue said as Ridge rounded the corner, a pair of police officers in his wake. Technically they had the power to arrest people, but it tended to cut through a few layers of inter-agency bureaucracy if they involved the police and let them do it instead.

"Hands where I can see them," Ridge said. He grabbed Nick's wrist and tossed him against the wall.

"What?" Nick said, confused. "Is this some kind of joke?"

"No, it's not a joke," Jane said. "They think you're a forger, a terrorist. You are in big trouble here, Nick. Huge."

"Is this for real?" Nick said, his smile beginning to slip.

"Nick, what did you do?" Jane pressed as the two officers frisked him, cuffed him, and read him his rights.

"A guy paid me to paint some artifacts for him," Nick said. "Why is that bad?"

"Did you do a canopic jar?" Jane asked.

"Among other things."

"Why didn't you tell me?" Jane asked.

"Because I thought you'd be mad, and rightly so, apparently. You've always had a hair trigger when it came to this kind of stuff, Jane, you know you have."

"Who was the guy?" Ridge asked.

"No idea. He found me on the internet. I had an ad out to do freelance artwork," Nick said.

"How much did he pay you?" Ridge asked.

"Five thousand dollars," Nick said.

"Five thousand dollars?" Jane echoed. "What were you thinking?"

"That I needed the money. Where else am I going to get that kind of cash, parking cars?" he asked. "I had the talent to do what he wanted, and I knew a bunch of stuff from listening to you talk all these years. So, really, it was kind of an homage to you and how much I listened and absorbed."

"Wait a minute, is that how you were able to afford my engagement ring?" she asked.

He shrugged. "I used some of it for that, and for some other stuff. It was good money, Jane. Come on, it wasn't that big of a deal."

"Not that big of a deal? You know how I feel about forgeries, that they're a scourge on my profession, and you knowingly did it anyway," Jane said. She was yelling now, but she didn't care. Nick still didn't realize how much trouble he was in, how wrong he'd been. And he'd used forgery money to buy the engagement ring he presented to her. She had never been more furious with him; she had never been more furious with anyone.

"So a few fakes slip in now and then. You're the only one who knows the difference," he said, and it was the complete wrong thing to say to her. She lunged for him, arms outstretched. Blue caught her around the waist, holding her off the ground as she struggled against him.

"Let me go, I need to hit him," Jane yelled, still reaching for Nick even as the officers led him away.

"Maybe take her somewhere, help her cool off," Ridge suggested, and he sounded amused.

"Right," Blue said, tossing Jane over his shoulder as he headed down the block.

After Nick was out of sight and they'd gone about a hundred feet, she began to calm down. "Of all the idiotic things he's ever done, that's the most idiotic. I think that hurt more than when he cheated on me. To think he purposely faked my life's work."

"You're more upset about that than the engagement ring?" Blue asked.

"Yes."

"So I guess this means the wedding's off," he said with repressed glee.

"There never was a wedding," she replied, sighing. "You can put me down now, I'm fine."

"Nope," he said. He continued to carry her like a flour sack until they reached his car. Then he set her down, pressed her against the car, and mashed his body to hers. "I hope I never make you that angry."

"You already did," she told him, though it was hard to remember when he was full on pressed against her, his face mere centimeters from hers.

"When?" he asked.

"When you walked away from me six months ago and never looked back," she said.

"I had some things I needed to work on."

"Did you work on them?" she asked.

"I'm here, aren't I?" he said.

"I thought you were here for work," she reminded him.

"Who do you think brought you on this project? I made a convincing argument that we couldn't do it without you," he said. "Are you really not getting married in two weeks?"

She shook her head. "Emily is getting married in two weeks. That was her dress you saw me wearing."

"Why didn't you correct my assumption?" he asked. He took her hands, pressing their palms together and winding his fingers through hers.

"How could you believe I was marrying Nick when you..." she trailed off.

"When I what?" he prompted.

"Exist," she said. They stared at each other, their breathing labored, their heartbeats synced and thumping out of control. Blue's phone buzzed with a text.

"I have to get that. It could be a work crisis," he whispered, pulling the phone from his pocket. He read the text and puffed a laugh.

"What?" Jane asked.

He turned the phone to show her a text from Maggie.

FYI, Mic's still hot.

"Who's Mick?" Jane asked.

"Not Mick, microphone. You're still wired, it's still on, and they're still listening."

She squeezed her eyes closed. "How do we turn it off?"

"There is no off. It has to be contained," Blue said.

She reached into the bodice, ripped off the microphone, and handed it to him. He tossed it in the back seat of the car. "Can you hear us now?" Blue asked, and there was no answering text from Maggie.

"Safe," Jane said.

"Safe," Blue agreed. "Now where were we? Oh, I remember." He cupped her face in his hands. "Missed you, Jane. So much."

Her hands rested on his chest, and she stood on her toes, bringing her lips closer to his. "I think maybe we need to go somewhere and have a long, thorough discussion."

"I'm a huge fan of that plan," Blue agreed when someone stepped behind him and spoke.

"Let's all go somewhere," the newcomer said as he jabbed a gun in the back of Blue's head.

CHAPTER 29

Jane didn't see the gun, she merely saw Charles standing by. "What are you doing here?"

"Taking matters into my own hands," Charles replied.

"What?" Jane asked, confused.

"Pretty sure we found our forger," Blue said.

"Charles wouldn't…" Jane began, but then she saw the gun.

"Charles would, and Charles did," Charles said.

"You're the forger?" Jane said.

"Let's all take a little ride, and I'll tell you my tale," Charles promised. "Jane, you drive." He marched them a few spaces away to his car, gave Jane the keys, shoved Blue into the front seat, and hopped into the back. "No buckle," he added when Blue reached for his seatbelt.

"I'm buckling," Jane said, her tone defiant as she snapped it into place.

"You can buckle, Janie," he agreed. He also didn't buckle and Jane made a mental note of the fact before starting the car and easing onto the roadway.

"Start from the beginning," Jane commanded.

"We'd have to go back too far for that. The point is I began to feel the need to right some wrongs, but to do that I needed money. The most expedient way to get it was to do what I did best, fake a few artifacts and sell them."

"You funneled money to terrorists," Jane said.

"They are not the terrorists. The United States government are the terrorists. I've seen things, Jane. Way more than you have or ever will. You know what it was like in Africa, the corruption, the brutality. I remained friends with people I knew when I was a mercenary, and things only got worse for them. I wanted to help, to do my part."

"But, Charles, you forged things you've spent your life investigating," she said.

"But that's not my life's work, it's not the most important thing. Don't you understand, Janie?"

"No, I really, really don't," Jane said, sniffling.

"Ugh, don't cry, please. Look, I promise not to off him in front of you, okay? I wouldn't want you to have to see that," he said. He reached out to smooth his hand on her arm, but she jerked it out of reach.

"Don't touch me," she snapped.

He withdrew his hand. "Hey, I'm mad at you too, you know. I fooled everyone until you came along and ruined it. It never occurred to me you would get involved with the government, with the way things are with your dad. Why did you?"

"Because they asked, and it was the right thing to do," she said.

He blew out a breath. "The right thing to do. You have wrong ideas about who the bad guys are in this scenario."

"Pretty sure it's the guy holding a gun and kidnapping me. Speaking of which, you ordered the first hit on me, didn't you?"

"Yes, but I was specific about not hurting you."

"And when we were having dinner with you and someone shot out the window and followed us, what was that about?" Jane asked.

"It was the ideal time to try and take you, but I swear I never wanted to hurt you. I wanted you off my trail, not killed," Charles said. "You know I care about you, Jane. We go back a ways, and you're one of the good ones."

"But you're not," Jane said, sniffling again.

"Don't say that," Charles said, sounding wounded.

She stopped at a red light and turned to face him. "How can you say you're good when you're talking about killing Blue?" As she spoke, she reached her right hand to the latch of Blue's seatbelt and tapped it repeatedly until he took notice. She kept eye contact with Charles as Blue surreptitiously began easing out his belt, stretching it across his waist and heading for the clasp.

"It's a necessary evil, but I promise you I'll do it quick and painless and then you and I..." he trailed off.

"What? What is the end of that sentence, Charles? You'll let me go, knowing what I know about you? We'll ride off into the sunset together? You'll have Sunday dinner with my family like the old days? Or you'll have to kill me, too?" She held his eyes. He gave her a sad smile.

"This is hard for me, it's wrenching, but it's not my fault. You've stumbled into something you had no part of, and you've become a liability," he said. "But the same goes for you. I'll make it quick and painless."

"My father will kill you, and he won't make it painless," she promised.

"I know, but he'll have to catch me first, and I won't make it easy," Charles said.

"He will catch you, and he'll kill you himself with his bare hands," Jane said.

Charles didn't reply, but Blue thought he saw a shudder pass through his body. Three things happened then. The light turned green, Blue clicked the latch on his seatbelt, Jane mashed her foot to the accelerator, jerked a hard right, and wrapped the car around a utility pole.

For a second, everything froze. Jane came to first; she was slightly stunned but not unconscious. She had been expecting the crash, but even so it left her dazed and shell-shocked. There had been a sound right before they hit the pole, a loud bang. With nothing short of panic, she inspected Blue to make sure he was alive.

He was. He had a strong pulse and was breathing fine. There was no visible blood on him, but he was unconscious, his head lying against the cracked window, a giant goose egg already forming on his skull. In the back, Charles began to stir. The only one not wearing his seatbelt, he had been tossed haphazardly to the left side of the car, but that worked in his favor, the thick seat doing its best to cushion him from any impact or trauma. Jane reached into Blue's jacket and pulled out his gun. She had watched Ethan handle it earlier, absently noting the lack of a safety. It was ready to go. All she had to do was use it.

Charles opened the door and spilled out onto the pavement. Jane opened her door and tested her legs. They were wobbly, but they worked. Charles was heading away from her, gun in hand. She was a bit panicked he was heading around the car, toward Blue.

"Stop," she called, raising the gun and taking aim. Her left arm didn't want to cooperate, but, being right handed, she didn't much need it.

Charles did as she did, turning to face her, his gun slack.

"Drop your gun," Jane commanded.

"Can't do that, Janie," he said. His hand tightened on the trigger, but he made no move to raise it.

"Drop it," Jane warned again.

"Come on, Jane. Are you going to kill me, really? You couldn't even kill bugs when we were kids."

"Of course I'm not going to kill you, Charles," Jane said, her mind flashing back to something Maggie had said. "But if your aim is good enough, you don't have to take the kill shot."

His eyes flashed with disbelief, followed quickly by fear and anger. He raised his gun, and she shot him in the right shoulder, forcing him to stumble back a step and drop to the ground in misery, the gun flying far afield of his fingers.

I should go and get it, Jane thought. She took a step, stumbled, and stopped short. Her eyes were drawn to her left side where blood poured from an open wound in her shoulder. *Oh, I was the one who was shot in the car,* she thought, almost remotely. "I always thought it would hurt more," she whispered, and then the shock began to ebb and the pain slammed into her, knocking her to her knees.

"Hurts, doesn't it?" Charles asked. He was on his knees across from her, panting from the pain of the wound she'd caused him.

"A lot," she replied.

"I'm not certain I would have been able to go through with killing you. You were always in my soft spot," Charles gasped, falling forward, his palms scraping roughly on the pavement.

"Pretty sure I could have killed you," Jane replied. Charles barked a harsh laugh, and it was the last thing she remembered before everything faded to black, like a heavy curtain being closed at the end of a play.

CHAPTER 30

Jane woke in the hospital. That didn't happen like she thought, either. She always imagined being pulled from somewhere else, a great foggy distance. In reality she snapped instantly alert, one minute unconscious, the next awake and in tune to what was happening around her.

She was hooked to an IV and monitor, and it was daylight. Nothing was in her throat, though it was a bit scratchy, as if she'd been intubated at some point. The IV felt vaguely uncomfortable, but she felt no pain, thanks to whatever was dripping benignly into her veins. She was alone in the room, and she was thirsty. *Looks like I'm all caught up,* Jane thought. Her most pressing concerns were Blue and Charles, in that order. Was Blue okay, and was Charles in jail? She had the horrible suspicion Charles had somehow managed to weasel away and escape, though she hoped against hope it wasn't true.

As if thinking of him caused him to appear, Blue entered her room wearing his own hospital gown, though he wasn't hooked to any monitor or device. "Jane," he said, hobbling forward. He stopped by her bedside, gingerly leaned in and kissed her on the lips. Jane took the hand that wasn't hooked to a monitor or IV and used it to draw him close, returning his kiss with as much interest as she could muster, which must have been a lot because eventually he broke it off and rested his head on her uninjured shoulder.

"I guess you're doing okay," he gasped.

"How are you?"

"Good. On concussion protocol for a week. Some things are a bit mixed up in my brain, but a bonk on the head will do that. Hopefully with a bit of rest things will clear up." He sat in the chair beside the bed. "I have some bad news."

"What?" Jane croaked, steeling herself for the worst.

"They had to do a bit of repair work on your shoulder. Your pitching career is over."

"Just when I was getting good," Jane said. "What about Charles?"

"He tried to get away, but the poor dope had a shoulder injury that left a trail and led us right to him. Let's say he's in federal custody and will be for a long, long time." He picked up her hand and pressed it to his cheek. "My poor Janie. I can't believe you got shot."

"I can't believe I shot a man, and you missed it," she said.

"For the record, that was a new gun. And you've now fired it more times than I have, and definitely hit more targets," he said, and she laughed. He took her hand and held it gently. "Are you too sick and weak to have our long overdue conversation?"

"Yes, but if you don't talk right now, I'll hunt you down and beat you with my IV bag," she threatened. "Start six months ago."

"First I realized meeting you was the magic cure to getting over Maggie. Next time I saw her after I dropped you off it was like seeing a pal, nothing more, certainly no inappropriate or unrequited crush. I'm happy to say it hasn't returned in the months since. At six months free, I think I'm officially cured and over her."

"Congratulations," Jane said. "Now get to all those other women you dated."

"Right, that. I met a few dates online and did my usual amount of research. I went into those dates fully armed. With one woman I even looked at her dental records."

"There'd better be an *and* here," Jane said.

"There is. *And* it was horrible. So incredibly boring. Once you pointed out to me how wrong and invasive it was for me to do that much poking around in people's private lives, I couldn't unsee it. I felt creepy and kind of ill and, did I mention, so incredibly bored. There was no mystery, no excitement, no sense of wonder or anticipation. I missed my Jane, who is a complete and utter mystery to me, a total question mark." He pressed her palm to his lips. "Jane, my Jane, I don't care anymore about your past. I don't care who you are or where you came from or that you have no virtual footprint, or that your dad is likely some terrifying criminal warlord. I want to be with you, up to and including forever. I love you."

"Blue, you are so incredibly much wow," Jane said and groaned. "That was supposed to be poetic and charming."

"You're on a lot of heavy duty drugs," Blue said, his tone sympathetic.

"Yes, but you know it wasn't the drugs. You know it was the awkwardness that inhabits my life."

"I do know, and I find it all kinds of adorable," Blue said.

"I so badly want to kiss you, but I also so badly want a sip of water," Jane said.

Blue stood painfully to his feet, hobbled to the sink, and brought her a drink of water. "Thank you," Jane said, dribbling water down her chin in her attempt to drink.

Blue brushed the hair away from her face, and they spent a minute looking at each other in that adoring way that only new love brings, until a shadow fell in the doorway, announcing someone's presence. Blue turned and saw his boss, rather his boss's boss, Colonel Caruthers. He dashed to his feet, repressing a groan of pain.

"Colonel, sir," Blue blurted. He was beyond shocked. The Colonel always dealt with Ridge. Except for when he first sprang him from prison all those years ago, Blue couldn't remember a time when the man had come specifically to see him. "This is Jane Dunbar, sir."

"As you were, Blue," The Colonel replied. Then, noting that Blue continued to stand, albeit wobbly, snapped, "I said sit, son."

Blue sat.

"As for the young lady, I'm familiar. And it's *Dr*. Jane Dunbar." He went forward and took Jane's hand. "How's it going, Princess?"

"Pretty well, Daddy," Jane returned, and Blue slumped forward onto the bed in an unconscious heap.

Jane sighed. "I was afraid of that."

The Colonel reached behind her for the remote, pressed a button, and spoke to the nurse's station. "We're going to need some smelling salts in room 308." He set aside the remote and resumed his hold on Jane's hand. "Tell me quick before he wakes up, do you really like him?"

"Yes," Jane said. "I do, lots and lots."

"Good because he's the best computer guy we've got, and it would be a real shame to make him disappear."

Jane laughed and then sniffled. "Dad, Charles."

"I know, honey. That was a blow to all of us, but not wholly unexpected. I tried to put a stop to it when he joined that band of mercenaries all those years ago, but I was in the states, and you guys were still in Africa." He sighed and pushed the hair out of her face, much the same as Blue had just done. "I missed so much because of this blasted job, Jane."

"Your country needed you," Jane said.

"So did my girls," The Colonel replied.

"We did fine, Dad. We always understood."

The nurses rushed in, looking at Jane askance. She pointed to Blue, still slumped in a heap on her bedcovers. They fled to his side, snapped open a plastic container of salts, and placed it under his nose. He came to immediately, staring around in bewilderment.

"Let's get you back to your room," one nurse said.

"Can't you leave him here please?" Jane said, patting the bed beside her.

"No, he shouldn't even be..." the nurse who was clearly in charge began, but The Colonel interrupted.

"Leave him here."

The nurses deposited Blue on the bed and scurried out of the room.

"Doing okay, Blue?" The Colonel asked.

"I don't know," Blue said, his wary gaze traveling between Jane and her father. They ignored him and focused on each other, letting Blue's bruised brain try to have a moment to catch up.

"I like the hair," The Colonel said, touching Jane's new Pixie 'do. "It's very you. Although the color, hmm." He cast a half-accusing glance at Blue who shrank back against the bed as if afraid The Colonel might reach out and strike him at any moment.

"And Blue's a blond," Jane said. "Who knew?"

"I knew," The Colonel replied. "Blue and I go back a ways, approximately ten tattoos and several bottles of color ago."

"Really?" Jane asked, looking between them.

"It's a story for a later date," The Colonel said. "In the meantime, we have something to discuss, girly. Is it true you stole a car and drove it to the airport?"

"Yes, sir," Jane said meekly.

"Did you hotwire it?" The Colonel asked.

Jane shook her head. "Screwdriver in the ignition."

The Colonel sighed. "And what would have happened if you hadn't been able to find an old enough model for that to work? Jane, I've been telling you for years, you have got to work on the hotwiring."

"I know, Dad, but it's not exactly an easy skillset to practice," Jane said.

"I'll get you something to practice on."

"Am I still unconscious?" Blue asked.

"A woman needs to know how to take care of herself, don't you agree, Blue?" The Colonel asked.

"No worries on Jane's front, sir. She's doing all right," Blue told him.

The Colonel leaned in, lowering his voice conspiratorially. "Did she really pepper spray you?"

"Sometimes when the light's dim, I still can't read small print and my eyes water," Blue told him, and The Colonel laughed, a rusty, ill used sound that was more alarming than endearing.

"I would pay good money to have seen that," The Colonel said, wiping his eyes. He checked his watch. "I have a meeting, but I wanted to tell you two things before I go. First, your sister is coming to see you."

Jane tensed and then winced. "Which one?"

"Both."

"Oh, Dad, no. Can't you tell them I'm not up for it?"

"Jane, you girls don't see each other often enough as it is. You got shot, honey, I think you can tough out one visit with your sisters."

"Getting shot was easier," Jane muttered, but The Colonel ignored her.

"Also, your mother wants you to come to dinner on Sunday."

"Tell Mom I'd be delighted." Jane paused. "What day is it?"

"Monday. You lost a day," The Colonel replied. She had come in late Saturday night, had long and tedious reconstructive shoulder surgery on Sunday, and slept until just a short while ago. The Colonel kissed her, stood to go, paused, and turned back. "Blue, we'd like you to come, too."

"Sure," Blue stuttered. "Thank you, sir."

"Hmm," The Colonel replied, giving him one more penetrating look before turning and walking out the door.

"So you're dad's The Colonel," Blue said when the man was safely away.

Jane sighed. "Yes. We use my mom's maiden name for safety's sake. And the lack of a footprint thing, well, you know better than anyone that being on the grid makes me traceable, and we're all high value targets because of his job."

"He's going to make a suit from my skin, isn't he?" Blue asked.

"Only if we break up."

"I guess I'm in the clear then," he said. "Does Ridge know who your dad is?"

"He's known from the beginning. My dad was the one who suggested me for the assignment," Jane said.

"So all this time he's been laughing at me."

"Probably a lot, but it's not his fault. I'm sure my dad swore him to secrecy. Most people don't even know he has kids," Jane said.

"Huh," Blue said, shifting to put his arm around her. It was likely he stunk, having been well over twenty four hours since he showered, but he didn't care. Jane stunk, too. He had seen her sick, shot, bloody, unconscious, asleep, with morning breath, with hospital breath, with makeup, with no makeup, before a makeover, after a makeover, in her element, out of her element, awkwardly bumbling, fluently speaking multiple languages, and so nervous at his touch she ran into a wall. And he liked her in every capacity he'd witnessed. No, he loved her. She was incredibly imperfect, and so was he, and he was deliriously in love with her.

"Also, you're right," he continued. "I would not have been able to handle that information in the beginning. I would have run away screaming."

"And now?" she prompted.

"I'm still screaming, but I'm running toward you."

"Perfect," she said. Her IV hand rested on his stomach as she tipped her face up to kiss him. The motion caused pain to shoot through her injured shoulder, but it was worth it. He kissed her in return until two new voices interrupted them.

"Nick's here," the first woman said.

"That's not Nick," the second woman replied.

"It's New Nick," the first woman said.

"New Nick is cute," the second woman said.

Jane pulled away from Blue, and forced her eyes open. "Hey, guys."

Two women stood in the doorway. One wore a marine uniform. The other was approximately Jane's height but fuller figured with a perpetually cheery expression.

"Hey, Janie," the marine one said. "How's the wound?"

"Hurts," Jane replied.

"I baked cookies," the plumper one said, holding a box aloft.

"Thank you."

"Are you going to introduce us to New Nick?" the cookie one asked.

"If I have to," Jane replied. "These are my sisters. Bailey's the one in uniform, and Poppy is the baker. Guys, this is Blue Bishop."

"How very alliterative it is to meet you," Bailey replied. "What happened to Old Nick, the rat fink?"

"He's still a rat fink," Jane replied.

"Want me to kill him for you?" Bailey offered.

"Maybe," Jane said.

"Wait, Old Nick is available?" Poppy said, and Bailey jabbed her in the arm.

"You can't date Old Nick. Respect the Code."

"I'm not a soldier," Poppy said, rubbing the arm Bailey had jabbed.

"The sister code, you little weasel. Don't make me punch you again," Bailey threatened.

"Jane doesn't care if I date Old Nick, do you Janie?" Poppy asked.

"Only on the basis that I think you could do a lot better," Jane replied.

"What does New Nick do?" Bailey asked, regarding him with eyes so much like her father's it was spooky.

"Computer stuff," Blue answered.

"He works for Dad," Jane added.

"Oh," Bailey and Poppy drawled, assessing Blue with new regard.

"I didn't know we were allowed to date people who work for Dad," Poppy said. "This opens up a whole new world of possibilities. Who else do you know, New Nick?"

"Do not set Hurricane Poppy up with people you want to remain friends with," Bailey warned, and now it was her turn to dodge Poppy's blow.

"You guys are making a great first impression, thanks," Jane said.

"We'll make an even better one on Sunday," Bailey promised.

Jane groaned. "No, you guys are going to be there, too?"

"And miss roasting New Nick? Not a chance," Bailey said.

"Shame about Old Nick, though. We just got him broken in," Poppy said.

"You mean you just got him broken," Jane interjected.

"What's the difference?" Bailey asked. Her watch beeped and, like her father a few minutes ago, she glanced at it with a sigh. "I have a meeting. Take care, kiddo. It was nice to meet you, New Nick. Oh, by the way, Charles ever gets free, I'm going to murder him."

"She's not joking. She made a detailed plan in her agenda on the way here," Poppy added. "See you, New Nick. Bring a friend on Sunday. I'm too desperate to be picky, and I'm an amazing pastry chef."

"Both true," Bailey agreed, putting Poppy in a headlock as they turned and headed down the hall.

"And those are my sisters," Jane said. "You can run away screaming now, if you like. I won't judge you."

"How about if we hobble away together to recover for a while instead," Blue suggested.

"Just you and me?" Jane said hopefully.

"You and me and hot water bottles and prescription-strength ibuprofen."

"Oh, baby," Jane said, tipping her face to kiss him again.

Blue started to respond and then pulled away. "You don't have any more family that's going to show up and terrify me right now, do you?"

"I have an aunt who can dislocate all of her appendages, but you probably won't meet her for a while. I'll save it 'till Christmas," Jane promised.

"Something to look forward to then," he said, reaching for her and finally kissing her without interruption for a good, long time.

*T*hank you for reading *The Mouse and the Maestro,* the third book in the Spies Like Us series. For further reading, please see www.vanessagraybartal.com

ABOUT THE AUTHOR

Vanessa Gray Bartal is a foodie who spends her time trolling bakeries and dreaming of new ways to use sourdough. When she is not baking (or eating), she loves to make music and spend time with her husband, three children, and sheepadoodle in rural Ohio. Her dream is to fill her books with enough coziness and warmth to brighten someone's day and make them smile. She would love to hear from you on Facebook or through email.